Ordinary Genius

FLYOVER FICTION   Series editor: Ron Hansen

Thomas Fox Averill

Ordinary
Genius

For Peggy —
with the pleasure of
our annual gatherings
on the North Shore, and
with admiration for your
continuing work —
Love, Tom

University of Nebraska Press

Lincoln and London

Designed and typeset by Richard Eckersley in Adobe
Minion Multiple Master with display in Bitstream
American Typewriter. Printed by Thomson-Shore, Inc.
⊗

Library of Congress Cataloging-in-Publication Data
Averill, Thomas Fox, 1949–
Ordinary genius / Thomas Fox Averill.
p. cm. – (Flyover fiction)
ISBN 0-8032-1068-x (cloth : alkaline paper)
1. Kansas – Social life and customs – Fiction. I. Title.
II. Series
PS3551.V375073 2004   813'.54–dc22   2004018195

For
Jeffrey Ann Goudie,
always
all ways
again

but the ordinary is the miracle.

Ordinary love and ordinary death,
ordinary suffering, ordinary birth,

the ordinary couplets of our breath,
ordinary heaven, ordinary earth.

Derek Walcott, *Tiepolo's Hound*

Contents

Acknowledgments

Thanks to all the editors who published these stories in their original form – acceptance and encouragement, along with careful editing, kept me believing that my short fiction would continue to find an audience.

My agent, Stephanie von Hirschberg, continues to support my work with the necessary balance of encouragement and criticism.

I am lucky to work at a place that understands my needs and nature. Washburn University of Topeka has been generous with grants, release time, and travel money to help me in the writing side of my academic life. My colleagues, too, are encouraging and perceptive.

Wichita artist Clark Britton sent me rich drawings to work with in "Midlin, Kansas, Jump Shot." His creation of a fictional Kansas town brought me months of inspiration.

Eric McHenry remembered the lines from Derek Walcott's *Tiepolo's Hound*, about Camille Pissarro.

Family and friends continue to bolster my work and enrich my life.

Readers have kept me going with e-mails, letters, and phone calls. My deep thanks to all of you.

"Running Blind" appeared previously in *New Letters* 58, no. 1 (Fall 1991); *Show Me a Hero: Great Contemporary Stories about Sports*, edited by Jeanne Schinto (New York: Persea Books, 1995); and *Literature for Life and Work, Book 2* (10th level textbook), edited by Elaine Bowe Johnson and Christine Bideganeta LaRocco (Cincinnati: South-Western Educational Publishing, 1998).

"The Musical Genius of Moscow, Kansas" appeared previously in *Cimarron Review*, no. 115 (April 1996).

"The Onion and I" appeared previously in *Virtually Now: Stories of Science, Technology and the Future*, edited by Jeanne Schinto (New York: Persea Books, 1996).

Acknowledgments

"The Summer Grandma Was Supposed to Die" appeared previously in *American Way*, October 15, 1992, retitled "Snakebite"; *Kansas Alumni*, August/September 1994, retitled "The Long Road Home"; and *Great Plains Magazine*, Summer 1997.

"Shopping" appeared previously in *New Letters* 65, no. 2 (1999).

"The Man Who Ran with Deer" appeared in *Roberts Award Annual*, December 1989; *Sonora Review*, March 1990; and *Best of the West 4* (New York: W. W. Norton, 1991).

"Matty" appeared previously in *Cottonwood* 49 (Summer 1994).

"Topeka Underground" appeared previously in *Greensboro Review*, no. 50 (Summer 1991), and was winner of the 1990 *Kansas Voices* competition.

"During the Twelfth Summer of Elmer D. Peterson" appeared previously in *Farmer's Market* 7, no. 1 (Spring 1990); and *Prize Stories 1991: The O. Henry Awards*, edited by William Abrahams (New York: Doubleday, 1991).

"Bus" appeared previously in *Soundings East* 23, no. 1 (Fall/Winter 2000).

"The Bocce Brothers" appeared previously in *DoubleTake* 4, no. 1 (Winter 1998).

A Story as Preface

"Why do you do it?" he asks. I talk of feeling trim, breathing deep, of burned calories, heart rate, endorphins, of T-shirts – a lifetime supply after five years of organized runs. I talk of sky, sun, wind, earth, asphalt, concrete. "Will you take me sometime?" he asks. My friend is blind.

Week one, one mile: asphalt high-school track. His legs are longer than mine. We stutter, finding our stride, his hand at my elbow. I describe the curves, teach him to lean. By the back stretch he is winded. I close my eyes. "What's wrong?" he asks, but I say, "Nothing, you're just tired."

Week eight, three miles: asphalt park roads. We run faster now. I describe trees, the elegant rose garden, the zoo, the amphitheater, the incredible blue of early summer sky, clouds billowing like runner's breath. Eyes on the road, I anticipate gradual rises and falls, corners, patches of loose gravel, dead limbs. "Just another half-mile," I say when his breath shortens and his hand loses my elbow for a second. He grunts: "Tell me in time. Time means more than distance." I say, "Okay, four minutes or so to go."

Week twelve, five miles: country roads. His hand pushes my elbow, begging for speed. We climb hills as steeply pitched as ladders. I call out the views, lush green, hazy with humidity. Downhills we run so fast I'm afraid for him. "Let go," he says, "just let yourself move. Don't talk, I know where I am now." I breathe hard. We run faster than I ever have before.

Week fifteen, 10k: downtown, intricate concrete course. "How fast?" I ask as we wait for the gun. He stretches his long, sinewy legs, says, "As fast as you can." He is calm, confident. I weave us through the congestion of bodies. We race. With .2k left he leans against me, asks "Straightaway?" and I gasp "Yes," and he passes me, sprinting. Someone stops him at the finish.

From then on: he runs with faster companions. He tells me: "Want to improve? Running's inside you. Don't watch what's around you, pay attention to what's inside." He's right, but, free again, I slow down, enjoy the view.

1

The Musical Genius of Moscow, Kansas

Middle C
MOSCOW

Moscow, Kansas: as insignificant as one breath of air among a lifetime, a single dirt clod in a vast field, a falling meteor that is unnoticed. One short main street of alternating brick and wooden buildings, none more than two stories high. The Atchison, Topeka & Santa Fe Railroad depot. Grain elevator the tallest thing for miles. Stars and terrible weather in the vast sky overhead; underneath, the Largest Natural Gas Field in the United States.

C♯
KLINSKY

At the edge of Moscow lived a farmer and his wife. Klinsky was much too old, Mamie Tull much too young. He was dirty, overalled, straw-hatted, with teeth still stained from years of tobacco. He had married – in desperation or charity, Moscow couldn't decide – Mamie Tull, fifteen, pregnant by God only knew whom. "Took advantage of the situation," some folks said, "to get him a wife he'd never have got otherwise."

"*She* took advantage," others said, "to get rich."

Nobody knew if Klinsky had the money he was rumored to, but sometimes he worked his land and sometimes he did not, and he drove German cars before anyone else in western Kansas did, and he raised exotic birds: peacocks, guinea hens, doves, pigeons, Polish chickens.

"Closest thing we have to a zoo," some said.

"A dump for bird shit," said others.

D

BIRTH

One full moon, Klinsky's birds ruffled their feathers and cried out. The peacocks fanned their tails, each eye reflecting the moon. In the house, Mamie's forehead turned clammy. Her feet cramped. For six hours she breathed, moaned, screamed. Mamie was so young, and had been so pregnant, Klinsky had not touched her since their marriage in the Stevens County Courthouse. *She* was the child he had never had, yet she was *bearing* the child he had never had. At dawn, when the baby finally came, a thin wrinkled girl, Klinsky wept until his shoes were wet. His doves and pigeons strutted in the yard. The little Polish roosters crowed. A coyote, the moon over one shoulder, the gathering sun over the other, told the sky about hunger. Klinsky brought Mamie tea and shyly watched her nurse the child. She laughed then. "Your beard," she said. "It's turned white."

"It is only the dawn," he said. "And my glistening tears." He turned to her, an old man in overalls, and began to move his feet. He danced as he had once seen his father dance, with small steps, arms raised. *"Das Licht bricht an,"* he sang to the new day. *"Das Licht bricht an, der sonnenaufgang, das Tagelicht. Das Licht bricht an."*

Mamie was too tired to wonder where this voice came from; he delighted her with his dance. The baby, then Mamie, fell asleep.

As the sun rose, Klinsky's Polish roosters tucked their heads under their wings. The guinea hens looked like boulders in the drive. The peacocks put away their fans and shut their eyes, not bothering to fly onto the porch roof, or the line of elm trees in the lane. All day, while Mamie and the baby and all of his birds slept, Klinsky watched over them, protecting them, he thought, though from *what* he was not certain.

D#

HERMIONE

"I will call her Hermione," said Mamie at dusk.

"Hermione Klinsky." Klinsky sounded the name.

"No," said Mamie. "Hermione Tull."

"You know I will be her father. She will be my daughter."

Mamie said nothing. Hermione nudged her mother's breast.

"This is not what you wanted?" Klinsky asked. "That you be mine? That she be mine?"

"We're not like your birds," said Mamie, "to be fed and bred and shown. To adorn a farm."

"I do not own the birds," said Klinsky. "Any time, they can fly away. They are owned by the sky. By their wings. They stay because they want to." He went to the window to watch a dove land in the cupola of the barn. He began to hum a song from his boyhood, a sad melody his mother had used as a lullaby.

Mamie shifted Hermione to her other small breast. "I'm sorry, Klinsky," she said. "I want to stay, too. So will Hermione." She was amazed by the smile that split Klinsky's tangled beard. But she still said, "Hermione *Tull.*"

E

THE VISIT

When they heard the news, the few old women of Moscow who did not care that Klinsky had married late, and to a pregnant girl the age of their grand-daughters, made their visit. As was their custom, each brought a basket that held a freshly killed chicken, a loaf of bread, an egg, and a bottle of wine. "She is long," said one. "She will live to be an old woman."

"Short fingernails," said another. "She will speak her mind."

"Hair so thick," said a third. "She has already thought much."

Hermione fumbled for Mamie's breast. Her mouth, a perfect O, released a lilting cry somewhere between the call of a dove and the wheezing of the church organ in its highest register. "Already she sings," said the fourth old woman. "You bring her to me as soon as she walks. I will find how best she is to make music."

Klinsky shooed the women down the stairs and took their offerings to the kitchen. He cooked as he had seen his grandmother cook when his brothers and sisters were born. He dressed the chickens and stuffed each one with a loaf of bread, torn into tiny pieces and made soggy with the egg and half the wine. He put the birds into a huge roasting pan, doused them with the rest of the wine, secured the lid and baked them for hours. The house swelled with the smell, and when Mamie and Hermione awoke from a late afternoon nap they lay quietly in the thick air, waiting to be fed.

Mamie ate one chicken, then another, then returned to her bed with the bones. After Hermione nursed, Mamie cleaned the bones, then cracked the legs for their marrow. When she fell asleep, Klinsky removed the bones and rocked Hermione. He sang her song after song from when he was a child.

Mamie slept for two days, nodding dreamily when Klinsky took Hermione to her breast. Klinsky changed Hermione's diaper when she fussed, sang her back to sleep. At night, all alone, he danced by the window.

F

LULLABY

As soon as Hermione realized it was her own voice crying or moaning, laughing or sighing, she exercised it with great delight. By the time she began to walk she could sing with each of Klinsky's lullabies.

"Do you hear?" Klinsky asked Mamie. He sat on his bed, eyes gleaming, humming when he was not talking. "She knows the music. Everything in her head spills out perfectly, like a birdsong."

"She's not singing," Mamie said. "You think she is because that's what you want to hear." She turned in her bed to face this husband.

"It's in her blood," said Klinsky. He pulled his bony feet out of his boots and lay down on his bed. The ceiling lowered when Mamie turned off the lamp. He hummed a sorrowful melody, but the sound raised the ceiling to show Klinsky the stars amidst a pale moon just shrouded with clouds.

"What do you know about her blood?" Mamie whispered to the open sky.

"I am talking about her heart," insisted Klinsky. "About what pumps through her heart. About music that is like blood."

"*Your* heart," Mamie said. "*Your* music. You have been singing since she was born." Her voice lowered the ceiling again, and the room darkened.

Then they both heard Hermione, in her crib, singing her heart, a song as sad as Mamie's words about blood. While Hermione sang, Klinsky rose from his bed, stripped off his overalls and went to Mamie's bed. She made a place for him, let him climb in, nestled her head on his chest, his crinkly beard in her ear.

"Blood is for breeders," he whispered. "For horses, for cows, for chickens. We are a family, no? Does blood have to do with that?"

Mamie and Klinsky lay quietly while Hermione tried her voice, octave after octave, mouth open and closed, screeching like the peacocks, fussing like the chickens, cooing like the doves. She sang a lullaby, and first Mamie's breathing, then Klinsky's, deepened into sleep. When they awoke before dawn, in the same bed, a deep silence surrounded them. They found each other, gently, quietly. And when they finished moving together, Klinsky wept. Mamie's fingers fluttered across his back. Hermione woke up and crowed at the rising sun.

F#

THE CHOICE

Dijka was the old woman who wanted to learn how best Hermione might make music. When the child was three years old, Klinsky took her to the old woman's house, where each room was a separate section of the orchestra: strings in the parlor; brass in an upstairs room; woodwinds in her bedroom; percussion in the basement, squatting like toads. The open attic windows let in air and birds, let in whatever Moscow, Kansas, sang in its rotation of days.

The piano in the front hall was the first instrument Hermione saw. She climbed onto the bench and began sounding the notes, listening to each one as though it were a new friend being introduced. Dijka sat beside her. Klinsky stood just inside the door. An hour passed before Hermione had struck each key, listened to each note. Dijka stood up.

"Tomorrow she will choose her instrument," Dijka said. "You will not stay."

When Klinsky told Mamie he would leave Hermione with the old woman, she shook her head. "I'll go. Somebody must be there."

Dijka met them at the door. Hermione ran by the old woman and found her favorite note on the piano. She sounded it once. When Mamie asked to come in, old Dijka said, "Not even *I* may go in. She must make her choice alone."

"She's too young to make choices," said Mamie.

"Did you listen?" asked Dijka. "She chose to play but one note. Each day she makes one thousand choices. You are the mother, yes, but who chose that? Did you? Perhaps she?"

Hermione climbed down from the piano bench and disappeared into the house.

Mamie saw nothing but darkness beyond the old woman's folded arms. She heard nothing, not the pizzicato of a violin string, not the bold declaration of the copper tympani, not the squawk of a clarinet reed, not the buzz of tiny lips in the mouthpiece of a French horn. She sighed. The spring sun warmed her back; the old screen door leaned against her with enough force to dot the flesh of her arm. "How long?" Mamie asked.

They waited in silence.

"She's not choosing," Mamie said.

"You are younger even than your daughter," said Dijka. "Perhaps you have lived by letting others choose for you."

"I *have* made choices," Mamie said. She wanted to repeat Klinsky's words, about flying away, about staying. She had chosen to stay.

"Shall we sit?" Dijka asked. "The porch swing is nice in the sun of the spring."

As the sun moved shadows, passersby came and went, wondering why Mamie Tull sat on Dijka's porch. The last passerby suddenly stopped still in the graded clay street and looked at the sky, amazed. Because Hermione was at the attic window, letting her voice find the wind, fly into trees, land on the street, haunt the porch, sound throughout all of Moscow, Kansas.

"The singers," said Dijka, "they find the highest open window. They breathe the sweet air and return the breath as an embellished gift. They never sit to perform. They must stand, and be seen." She stood up and offered Mamie her hand. "Are you prepared for such a life?" she asked.

Mamie could not speak, but she was not alone in that. All of Moscow was silent, listening. On his farm, at the edge of town, Klinsky stopped his work to smile.

.

G

PIANO TUNER

Dijka's neighbor, Czaslow, was the piano tuner. He was blind. But he saw each note as a shape, palpable in the air. He was warming soup when Hermione's voice illuminated his house. To him, this voice was more than music: it was light, revealing something about sound that he – a man who lived by sound – had never known. Each note was an essence. As Czaslow listened, he was ashamed: for every poorly tuned piano; for every imperfect note shaped in his mind; for his blindness to what each note was meant to be. His knees buckled, the chicken soup foamed over on the stove, and Czaslow lay stunned on his kitchen floor.

The next day, Dijka slapped his face with hands cupped full of cold water. "Come," she said. "You must tune my piano."

Not remembering why he lay in a stupor, Czaslow took Dijka's hand. She hurried him next door. In the hall, Czaslow heard more than Dijka's breathing. Someone stood next to the piano. Two others breathed in the kitchen. "The piano is not in tune," Dijka complained, "though you adjusted it only last month. Listen." She played middle C. To Czaslow it sounded like middle C; it looked round, whole, vibrating like a small pool of water in a gentle rain.

"You rushed me from my home," he said. "I must have my tuning fork." As he backed away his foot caught a chair in the hall. The chair leg, scraping the old flooring, made a sound like middle C as sung by a hoarse rooster.

9

"I want no fork," said Dijka. "I want my piano tuned to this voice." She beckoned to Hermione, who cocked her head and opened her lips. Hermione was thin, her small body unmuscled, but she stood erect, as aware of what sound she must make as the crafted pipe of a cathedral organ some builder had spent a lifetime perfecting. And when she sang middle C, Czaslow remembered his delight, his shame, his swoon. He stumbled forward, opened the lid of Dijka's piano, and found the tuning socket. As Hermione's voice hummed in his head, he adjusted middle C, turning the small peg slightly clockwise, only about the thickness of an eggshell. But it was the same difference the shell makes for a growing embryo: the difference between life and death, between air and water.

"Next," he shouted, and Hermione sang the octave. Then the octave lower. Each time Czaslow shouted "next," Hermione sang the note he needed to hear, until the piano stretched and settled into a perfect roundness, as full and fragile as an egg, a perfect egg of sound that Czaslow had never seen in his head before. He sat exhausted, as though *he* had been played rather than the piano. His huge white eyes, one looking up, the other down, floated in tears. Dijka called Klinsky and Mamie from the kitchen. They were shocked by Czaslow's look of tortured ecstasy. "I cannot, I *must* not, tune another piano without your daughter," Czaslow said.

Dijka nodded. "It is a good practice for her voice. Let them go to each piano in Moscow."

"Yes," Klinsky said. "Let each home know what music might be."

So, all through the next month, Hermione and Czaslow went from house to house, in Moscow and out into Stevens County. Talk of them spread so quickly that people hoped for them long before they arrived. No matter where – rich homes or poor – they were greeted happily. Before they finished any piano, they had an audience of neighbors, and they had eaten pastries and drunk tea.

Czaslow gained ten pounds. He spent his evenings exhausted in a chair, his waist unbuttoned and bulging. He wept uncontrollably. Each night he saw Hermione's voice in his head, but he could not sustain the clear shape of it, the perfection of its vibrations, the solid way it hummed when he was with her. It turned into his own raw voice, his own disjointed shape, and mocked all his days of imperfect tuning. He lived only for the sound of Hermione's voice, and yet, on the thirtieth day, when she came to his house at nine o'clock to call his name, he did not answer. He was dead. His imperfect heart had swollen and burst like an old piano string, left untuned too long. His tuning fork, brought from the old country but abandoned at the top of his piano, had disappeared.

G#

PIANO

Soon after Czaslow's death, Mamie and Hermione found Dijka at the piano, her head resting on the keys. When she rose up, B-flat still creased her old forehead. "I cannot always be with her," said Dijka. "You must learn, Mrs. Mamie, so you may accompany her."

Mamie covered her mouth at the thought. When she sat down beside Dijka, she had to reach over her pregnant womb to sound the keys. Dijka took Mamie's hand and curved her fingers. "You must touch the keys gently, with both care and knowledge. As though the ivory were Hermione's face."

From then on, as Hermione sang from the attic window, Dijka showed Mamie the keys, the scales, the timing of notes; Dijka added the left hand, in time with the right, then in syncopation. Mamie was young, an eager learner.

Klinsky cooked meals and maintained the farm. Outside, he sang through chores; inside he hummed, as though it were sound that swelled Mamie's belly. He did not care for breeding, but his eager voice sang one song: I, Klinsky, helped to make this child.

"Play," he told Mamie. "You must learn just as quickly as old Dijka ages."

Mamie played until her fingers were raw, then smooth with the thin calluses of hands that have a use. At first, she wasn't certain she would like the piano. Dijka had not allowed her a choice. When she said this, Dijka smiled. "Have you walked beyond the piano in this house? Your hands, do they wish to touch a viola string? Your lips miss the warm cup of a trombone mouthpiece? Or the numbing vibration of the oboe reed? You *chose* the piano."

Dijka patted Mamie's womb. Mamie felt such a tremendous kick that she lifted off the piano bench. "You see," said Dijka. "Is every choice something we think about?"

A
SHADOW

One day, in her ninth month, Mamie sat playing the piano Klinsky had moved onto the large screened porch on the north side of the farmhouse. Two peacocks stood in the yard listening. Inside, Hermione sang Susanna's *Deh vieni, non tardar* from *The Marriage of Figaro*, acting out the opera with dolls. Klinsky worked in the barn, transferring Buff-crested Polish eggs into an incubator. He hummed, first with Mamie's piano, then with Hermione's voice.

A sudden shadow in the barn door became a cracked voice: "I was happening by." A young man strode into the barn. "I heard the piano. It needs tuning."

"It is tuned to my daughter's voice," said Klinsky.

"Then your daughter's voice needs tuning." The young man reached into his pocket and brought out a tuning fork. He flicked his finger to sound the pitch, then held it to Klinsky's ear.

Klinsky heard nothing.

"This fork was given to me by Czaslow, just before he died," said the young man. "Do you see his initial on it?"

"The letter is for middle C," said Klinsky. "If you knew Czaslow, why do I not know you?"

"Do you know everybody? Everybody's kin?" The young man snatched the tuning fork back into his pocket. "Czaslow taught me to play piano." The young man looked out the door. "Someone is trying to play," he said. He laughed. "The child's voice isn't what he said it would be."

"My daughter's voice?"

The young man moved close to Klinsky. "So you know your own family, anyway?" he said. His mouth was too broad, his teeth too small, his breath pungent even among the other smells of the barn.

"Our piano needs no tuning. When my wife plays, when my daughter sings, it cannot be improved. Ask anyone in Moscow."

"Let's ask Dijka." When the young man left the barn, Klinsky followed. They walked through fields, the mile to Dijka's house. Only when they reached Dijka's porch did Klinsky remember he had forgotten to switch on the bulb in the incubator.

The young man made the screen door flap against the jamb before Dijka appeared in the dark hall. "I've come to play your piano," he said. He went inside and pulled the tuning fork from his pants.

When he knocked it against the mahogany piano lid, Dijka winced as though he had struck her. "Herman," she said, "has it not always been in tune?"

Herman played middle C. The tinny sound was not a note, it was a child beating a tarnished spoon against an aluminum pan with a hole in it. Dijka winced again. Herman sat down at the bench. Each note sounded more frightening than the last. "This instrument is old, like the people in this town," said Herman. He opened the lid and found the tuning socket. He beat the tuning fork against the piano again. He watched the hammer strike middle C. "Old woman," he laughed, "you're running a boardinghouse for mice. They've chewed the felt to pad their nest." From under the strings he pulled a handful of felt, hair, straw, and dust. He picked at it until he found a newborn mouse. "Here's your enemy." He pinched the little mouse between his thumb and forefinger, and let it drop to the floor.

Then he turned the tuning pegs until each octave was correctly spaced, until each string sounded correctly next to its partners. Yet to Klinsky it was like a Frankenstein: each part, taken for itself, could not be faulted, but the overall effect was monstrous.

"I'll reglue the felt tomorrow," said Herman. "And play it like old times."

Dijka sat dejected, the baby mouse at her feet. "I thought you were gone away," she said. A string in the piano snapped. Down the hall, a violin, as though tuned beyond the strength of its box, suddenly shattered, spitting out its center. Upstairs, an oboe reed cracked. A trumpet valve corroded beyond movement. In the attic, an old owl woke up, shrieked, and flapped out of the window. Dijka slumped to the floor. Even as he felt for a pulse, Klinsky knew she was dead.

Klinsky looked up at the young man. "All this time, I have been thinking more of joy than sorrow. Yet I knew the father of my child would return." Klinsky left Herman in Dijka's hall. Even before he reached his barn, he heard Mamie, her fingers finding each key where it should be. Then Hermione, still giving her voice to her play. Although their music was a beautiful gift, it saddened Klinsky.

In the barn, the eggs he'd gathered were cold. In his head Klinsky heard a song, a dirge, something from the old country, a lament for how the world can ignore the songs in the human heart. Klinsky began to hum, then to sing, that dirge. The eggs broke in his hands.

B♭

CHURCH BASEMENT

Within hours, everyone knew of Dijka's death. With each retelling of the news, another instrument in her house fell into disrepair. The men in the cafe spat coffee grounds back into their cups: "She was practically dust," and a trombone spit valve landed on a musty carpet in the northeast bedroom of the musical house. The women in the small grocery squeezed lemons to calculate their juice: "The last of the old school," and a viola bow cracked along its spine. Two farmers paid for gasoline at the dusty counter of the Co-op: "She was never in her right mind," and a glockenspiel rusted on its frame.

All of Moscow tried to remember Herman. Which of Dijka's students? Which of the boys who had accompanied Czaslow on his work?

And almost before they had finished whispering their conjectures, Herman would knock on their doors with the tuning fork. "Your piano," he would say, "is out of tune. My first tuning will be free."

Since "free" was seldom heard in Moscow, Kansas, and because they were curious, many let Herman into their homes. They could not tell whether he changed the pitch of their pianos for better or worse, but by the time Herman left, they had something to tell a neighbor.

"He sweated like Czaslow when he tuned the highest octaves."

"His fingers, when he played, had their own life, like they were not connected to his hands. Nor his hands to his arms."

"When I told him about Czaslow and Hermione, he wondered how a little girl could fool an entire town."

Klinsky heard these reports, and more, one Saturday night when he went to the Moscow Ale Haus for his weekly glass of beer. He had three more glasses and stumbled home in the moonlight, his shadow dancing ahead of him, as though mocking the joy he had felt these few years. Sweat soaked his clothing; he climbed the stairs in squeaky shoes and stood at Mamie's bedside. "All that you know, I must know," he said.

Mamie exhaled a trilling sigh, like a pigeon disturbed in its sleep. Klinsky lay on the floor and stared at the lowering ceiling. He might have been in a tomb. Mamie's voice washed over him. "He is Herman Battenfeld," she began, "from Ulysses."

Herman spent his boyhood with his fingers on the keys of his grandfather's piano. He hated school. His father was a drunkard, his mother a runaway. The piano was refuge, not strength; music was escape, not solace; life was suffering without redemption.

Mamie first heard his music in the basement of the Ulysses Methodist Church, where he nurtured his wounded self away from the others. She walked quietly down unlit stairs until she found him, his eyes closed. He was the saddest, most tortured-looking person she had ever seen, and her heart was moved. Her mind said, *genius.*

She put her hand on his shoulder, and he played a mad dancing slide down the length of the keyboard. When he pounded the lowest note on the old piano, he turned to her and said, "I have been waiting for you."

Mamie had never been addressed with such certainty. His scratchy voice was as urgent as the notes on the still-vibrating piano. She believed what he said. She continued to believe him when he talked of their life together after they found their destiny far from Ulysses and Moscow, far from southwestern Kansas. She fell in love, not so much with his words as with his need for her.

But after a year of meeting in sandy lanes, abandoned barns, empty silos, always speaking of what would be and then lying down together, Mamie grew tired of his need. The same night she readied herself to tell him she would no longer come to him, she realized she was carrying his child.

She wrote a simple note: *Why did I ever hear you play? Or listen to your voice? Why did I ever let you . . . ? Why did I think I loved you? I will always hate you.*

"I stayed home, indoors, for the next six months," Mamie told Klinsky. "Until you came for me. And then you gave me your happiness. And your music."

Klinsky said nothing. A piano sounded in his head, but he did not know who played it – Herman, Mamie, or his own mother, back in the old country. For all Mamie knew, he might have been asleep, or dead.

B

CONCERT

The next day, Klinsky rose from the floor at the first crow of his old Polish rooster. "He speaks ill of us," he said to Mamie. "We will go to Moscow." He loaded the piano from the porch onto his truck and called Mamie and Hermione from the house. They drove to town, blasting the horn at the Catholic Church, then the Methodist. They drove up and down every street, each one decorated with a scurf of stunted cottonwood trees, or half-dead elms. Klinsky's urgent horn pulled people from parlors and kitchens, drew them from mobile homes, from clapboard, stucco, and limestone houses. People wandered out of old tin garages or rotting barns. They climbed out of basements and root cellars.

Finally, Klinsky parked in the sunflowers and jimsonweeds on the south side of Moscow's eight-cylinder grain elevator. When Klinsky leaned against the truck horn for one last honk, the sound echoed up and out from the conjoined, concrete silos just as sound might move in the finest concert halls in Europe. Hermione began to sing, scales and octaves, warming up as Dijka had taught her. Mamie joined her on the piano. Together, they made a sound never before heard in Moscow, Kansas.

Birds came from all directions, making a black line on the edge of the

grain elevator, a red necklace on the power lines, a blue chain on the scrub-
by willows growing in the sunny creek draw. Then the citizens of Moscow
came. Some walked, with folding chairs and cushions to sit on. Some drove
their cars, shoved open their doors, and sat waiting.

Klinsky stood next to the piano, and Mamie stopped playing. Hermione
hummed through Klinsky's announcement. "Say, all of you," he began. "You
know me from years now. I have been in this same town, like most of you,
since I was born. My Mamie was born in this town, too. You know her."
Mamie played heavy chords with her left hand.

"You have had my daughter in your homes, some of you, when she came
with Czaslow to tune your pianos to her wonderful voice." Hermione sang a
note so high and pure that a window in the cabin of the elevator cracked.
And when she moved down from that note, the citizens of Moscow felt a
tingling in their spines; she played their vertebrae like xylophones. "We have
come to share ourselves, as we truly are," said Klinsky.

He sat down on the gate of his truck, then, and listened. Few of the people
knew the music Hermione sang, or the music Mamie made to accompany
the singing. Hermione sang the quick chirrup of the cardinal, and people
laughed; she sang the pure round voice of a dove, and tears sprang into people's eyes; she warbled and their hearts rose; a peacock's sad warning turned
hearts cold. As she sang, people felt things they had never felt before.

And Klinsky jumped off the truck bed and began to dance, slow at first, as
he'd danced the day Hermione was born, then faster, as he remembered the
songs she had sung to him and Mamie once she found her voice, and then
still faster as he remembered the quickening life in Mamie's womb, a life to
be born into the music of Moscow, Kansas.

As the people of Moscow heard Hermione's voice and saw Mamie's face,
radiant, and her hands, moving perfectly around the languid globe of her
womb, they wanted to join Klinsky's joyful dance: they knew life's sadness in
each mournful note, life's joy in each round note, life's fullness in how their
hearts filled, listening. Had Czaslow been alive, he would have known how
each person felt, for, upon hearing Hermione's voice, he had realized that
each note, as he had imagined it in his head, had been only the wraith of
sound, the ghost of what sound could be. Hermione's gift was not so much

to make music – to imitate the notes on one of Dijka's yellowing sheets – but to make others realize what music was. That is why Mamie was compelled to play, and Klinsky to dance, and the citizens of Moscow to gather through the spring afternoon in the weed-grown parking lot of the grain elevator.

Octave C
LONE BIRD

Like a shadow, Herman Battenfeld stood at the edge of the crowd. He muttered to whoever might listen. "She's *my* daughter," and an old woman waved him away in disgust. "I was *her* lover," and a young man turned from him. "Czaslow once called me a genius on the piano," and a family eating apples threw their cores at him.

Herman worked his way to the side of the crowd, breaking through sunflower stalks, until Klinsky saw him and stopped in his dance. Hermione's voice wafted onto the wind. The music of the piano gently turned away, as though Klinsky's truck were pulling out of town. Just before Herman spoke, the birds fluttered their wings.

"You have what is rightfully mine," he announced. "*My* love, *my* child, *my* piano."

"What do I have?" asked Klinsky. "I own nothing more than anyone in Moscow. This music? This dance I do? This wind, these birds, this sky? You may have it, too. Whatever you want, or whatever wants you."

Herman raised Czaslow's tuning fork in his left hand. "I want what is mine," he yelled. "Mamie, and Hermione. I want to play the piano. Let everyone listen, and hear music."

Klinsky lifted his arms. "Do you want to hear music?" he asked Moscow, Kansas.

Silence was his answer.

"So be it," said Klinsky. "And after you play what is in your heart, you may have whatever comes to you."

Mamie stood up from the piano bench and moved to the side of the pickup truck. Hermione joined her, face hidden in her mother's dress.

Herman climbed up and sat at the piano. Around him, the world paused:

bird, wind, and sky waited to hear Herman Battenfeld. He raised his hands above the keys, poised for the right moment. A mourning dove broke the silence. "There's music," shouted an old man.

Herman sighed audibly.

"Now he's playing the wind," said a rough voice in the front row of the crowd. Herman put his hands in his lap. When he lifted them again, someone shouted: "Play us the sky, Herman."

Herman sounded the keys then, but, dissatisfied, returned his hands to his lap. He tried again, but did not like the sound.

"Yes," shouted another voice, "play what's in your heart, if you can find anything."

Herman lifted his hands a final time. When he brought them down, it was to club the piano, beating the keys into contortions of sound that drove the birds, red and blue, shrieking into the sky.

Finally, Herman stood, tears in his eyes, in front of Moscow, Kansas. "I am the genius," he screamed. He jumped from the truck and ran through the crowd.

The black birds, and the gray, swirled in the sky like a bruise. They followed Herman, as though to see where he might go.

And then the citizens of Moscow went to their homes, hungry for the dinner they had given up to hear Hermione and Mamie. Klinsky stood quietly next to his truck until he was alone with his family. When he hugged Mamie and Hermione, Mamie felt the water in her womb break, and a quick stab of urgency from a new child who wanted to be born.

D.C. al Fine – FATHER

Mamie lay down in the back of the pickup truck. Since Moscow had no hospital, Klinsky went for the few old women who might help.

The child in Mamie's womb kicked, poked, and pounded. "Like a bag of cats," said one of the old women. Mamie felt strong and ready. She had chosen this one.

At Klinsky's farm, birds roosted on the house, settled in the yard. Peacocks screamed until the old women could hardly think. "Such a place," they whispered. "How to stand living with the filth of birds?"

"And him with such money."

"How to live with such a marriage, pregnant before, and someone else the father."

"And yet he is happy, and Mamie and Hermione so lovely."

"To make a baby at his age?"

"Has he not always been cracked in the head?"

"You should be so cracked, if so happy."

The women worked together through the night, Mamie hardest, and just as the day broke, the baby broke free of Mamie's womb: alive, strong, a kicking boy with a hairy head; a long-armed boy of touching hands.

When he filled his lungs and cried out, the sound was so unmusical that Hermione, and then Klinsky, and then Mamie, began to laugh.

Coda – WILL

Mamie let Klinsky name this baby, and he named it for his own father, Wilhelm Klinsky. They called the boy Will, and from the first Will knew what he wanted; when he crawled, Klinsky's birds fluttered ahead like litter showing the wind where to blow.

On his fourth birthday, Wilhelm's family started upstairs to sing "Happy Birthday." Will was not in his room, nor in the house, nor on the farm. "Is he not at Dijka's?" asked Klinsky. "As Hermione, at such an age?"

They heard the abandoned house before they saw it, as though someone were inside, tearing it apart: pounding woodwork, breaking dishes, dumping silver from drawers, tapping windows to see if they'd break, hammering at the old plaster between the studs. Dust rose from the house, billowed out the attic window. "He has discovered the percussion," said Klinsky.

And so he had. Klinsky and Mamie and Hermione moved all of Dijka's percussion instruments to Klinsky's barn loft. The next day, Dijka's house caved in on itself, the rubble filling the empty, rock-walled basement. Only one mouse was left alive to chew on a wooden xylophone, abandoned because it was missing middle C.

Will learned to drum the world. He watched the chickens strut and he punched their rhythm. He snared with a preening hen. A flowering peacock opened its eyes to the gradual stretching of a timpani. The sun rose to the mellow brushing of a tenor drum, set to the thrum of the bass. The moon was a bongo drum, deepest when full. Each season brought a rhythm, both new and old, to the pulsating, rotating earth.

Sound and rhythm found their center in Moscow, Kansas, radiating from the top of Klinsky's barn. Birds knew it first and circled above on straight wings, as though Klinsky's farm held them up.

Even now, birds of every kind perch on Klinsky's chimney. They fluff their feathers in the heat. They cock their heads, listening to the singing, playing, drumming, laughing, crying. Sometimes, as though remembering Herman Battenfeld, they fly away, shrieking, leaving the old farmhouse, and Moscow, behind.

People driving by on the highway think it fitting to see anxious birds. What a godforsaken place, they think. They keep driving, alone and afraid, reassuring themselves that nothing ever happens out nowhere, at the edge of Moscow, Kansas.

Fine

The Onion and I

My father was, I am sure, intended by nature to be a cheerful, kindly man. He had been raised, the son of farm people, in the state of Kansas. He rose early each morning, as though some irregular but insistent rooster still sounded in his head, as though restless stock waited for hay and oats, as though it might be best to get into the garden before the heat of a summer day peeled his skin again. He might have spent all his life happily bent to the rhythms of agricultural life, the hard work by day, the sound sleep by night, the sun in its seasons, the moon in its cycles, except that first his mother, and then mine, had ambitions for him: Grandmother matched his intelligence to a future at the university; there, he met Mother.

At university he found himself happiest doing simple things. He earned his tuition money each year selling onions, and nothing made him happier than watching onions grow: the limp slips of green he pinched into the earth stiffened into substantial, firm scallions, then began to swell at the roots, pushing at the soil – which my father kept pliant with his hoe. They added layer upon layer, pound upon pound of sweet flesh – white, yellow, red – until the green tops withered to gray and brown and my father knew that under the soil lay his wealth, happy to stay in the earth until whenever he might want to dig it up and deliver it to a local produce market.

"My hands," he told me, "would smell of onion juice for weeks. People looked at me oddly in Calculus."

All but my mother. She admired this quiet man, who smelled of earth and produce. She had been raised in a suburb and smelled of French lilac. She was an ambitious young woman, enlivened by whatever was in the air, whatever forced the barometer of opportunity up or down. Not even spring weather could keep up with her shifting studies at university: from psychology and its use in the corporate business world; to biology and how certain fungi might feed a growing world population; to physics, so that she might someday design rounded, energy-efficient dwellings; and on to computer science. Where she stayed. In the computer she found all the rest of the world.

My parents had a home page before they had a home. I believe history will support me when I say they were the first couple to be married in cyberspace. My mother had written a home page for herself, then one for my father. Then she linked them. She and my father were married in a chat room, with one of Mother's various chat groups as witnesses. An Internet minister of no particular faith sat at his keyboard and typed in the "Do you take this . . . ?" and my parents took turns typing "I do." My mother had downloaded graphics for the rings and the final kiss, and her chat group keyed in cheers, congratulations, and best wishes – everything but their tears.

The first venture into which the two people went turned out badly. My mother wanted to provide a wedding service for others on the Internet. Now, understand that these were the very early days of the system. The government – along with all the television networks and cable companies, and the huge telecommunications corporations, and the software giants, and the computer programmers, and the hardware companies, and even all of the visionary people like my mother – did not quite understand what the Internet, what the virtual world, what cyberspace would really become. Early life on the Internet was chaotic, sporadic, risky. There were all kinds of opportunities but no coordination. Perhaps an analogy will do: it was as though my father, growing onions, might have thousands of seed onions, yet have to plant them in fields miles apart, and then walk from field to field to see if they were responding to the soil; once a single onion grew, he might have to sit in his field and wait for someone to chance by in order that he might try to sell it.

Such was my mother's wedding service business. After she had helped marry a few others from her various chat rooms and bulletin boards, once she linked a few other home pages together, she settled down and waited for those people on line to find her. But it was hard to make a living. People cruised the Internet, read her pitch, looked over her graphics, listened to some of the variety of music to choose from, downloaded a dress or two, maybe an invitation, then roared away, ready to create their own weddings. Or people went through with one of my mother's ceremonies and then found themselves dissatisfied. They demanded she write a divorce page, complete with arbitration for alimony and custody.

Of course things like divorce, alimony, and custody were impossible in those early days. The court system was not on line. The government had plenty of information on what they liked to call the "superhighway," but no power of enforcement. Every user was a kind of renegade, invested with the superficial power to do anything and everything – from hacking credit to uploading pornography. Everyone was like a thief; no one was like the law. Almost anything could be done that could be imagined. And, almost anything could be undone: viruses ran rampant. In fact, it was the huge public computer health crisis that moved us more and more toward a centralized system, toward the virtual world so many live in today. After all, people wanted the same kind of protection on the information superhighway as they had on any of the interstates. Once the government, together with all the huge telecommunications companies, realized they could make and enforce laws on the computer, they also realized they could make and control people.

It is difficult to explain the leap into cyberspace as anything but a leap, though there were small steps, incredible preparations, years and years of readying people's minds and hearts for the experiment. Perhaps my mother and my father will serve best as an example of what happened. They were full of enthusiasm and dreams, energy and optimism, but they found themselves unable to become financially solvent in those early virtual days. They read pamphlets and manuals, they believed in the best in themselves and other people, just as so many Americans had before them. They spent more and more time on the Internet, making friends, visiting the vast array of home pages, learning how to shop from the big catalog companies, how to bank, how to find interesting entertainment – everything from films and television to music and soapbox orations – how to preview vacations and buy groceries. But it was a time of discouragement. For every wonderful opportunity, there were thousands of people instantly diluting its potential. For every exciting breakthrough, there was a system crash, a new virus, a bug. For every hope, there was despair. Many people, like my own father, longed for days of limited ambition and moderate success. It was in those days that I came wriggling and crying into the world.

That was also about the time when my mother heard about the first cyberlife experiments. They are well known now, but remember that this was before the cyberworld became *the* world, before those who followed my mother and father decided to take the great leap into virtual life. My mother was fascinated with those early projects. And she was ambitious that I have a different life from hers, or from my father's. And, of course, she had been interested in managing people, in feeding them on limited resources, in building structures for them to live in. So when the government announced Project Bidwell, wherein it would move a group of people *into* the computer, she convinced my father that this was *the* future, and, therefore, it was their future.

They moved into the virtual town of Bidwell and embarked in the business of helping the government perfect a cyberworld so seamless – or should I say so seem-full? – that nobody would feel dissatisfied living there rather than in what so many people so stubbornly insisted on calling the "real" world. Our move took six years, as we were interviewed, readied, deemed fit for the Bidwell experiment.

I remember getting rid of each of our possessions. I was but a boy, and attached to things in the way of a child. It is discouraging how people with so little in the world can grow so fond of each small thing. My mother insisted we were losing nothing, but by the time we entered our shelter, the size of a huge onion – like the Munchkin houses in *The Wizard of Oz* – we had given up everything we could touch. All that was ours – clothing, photographs of our relatives, pots and pans, souvenirs from our small travels, our automobile, even our pet dog, Sunflower – had been scanned in, re-created, had become virtual things in the Bidwell System.

You see, in a time of limited resources, it makes sense that people might have as rich a life in a computer as in that "real" world – even a richer life – and yet not use up, nor pollute, precious resources. Our experimental program fed us protein paks while we went to Bidwell's virtual restaurant and ordered from the menu, were served, smelled, and even seemed to taste the rich food that would have been so expensive to prepare and so dangerous to our bloodstreams to ingest. We could get into a virtual car and take any trip we wanted – the Bidwell System included the Oregon Coast, the Grand Canyon, even the long interstate drive across Kansas – and, of course, we used no gasoline, polluted no air; we did not wear out a single highway, not to mention the treads on our nonexistent tires. Think of a world in which one can do or use anything, and yet nothing is ever used up.

The Bidwell System, with its on-line town, citizens, and services, had not been written in a day, and it took many days to understand. But my mother, ever ambitious for us and for our future, rallied our spirits. We were pioneers, she said, in the great American tradition. The three of us sat side by side, helmeted, logged-on, keying and mousing our way through the cyberworld. We were the first astronauts of cyberspace. Mother's enthusiasm was so strong it might have been programmed into the computer, or flashed as an image into the helmet I wore to replace the sensory data of the "real" world with the sensory data projected by the computer. I was, after all, my mother's son. I don't know what was in my father's helmet, but sometimes he wearied of it. My mother shook her head disapprovingly whenever he took it off.

One day, he walked out of our small dome and sat on the ground. I followed him. I remember squinting, squeezing my eyes against the incredibly bright light of the sun. I approached him until my shadow fell over his bald head, which was as bare and white as an onion. He looked up at me as though he wasn't certain who I was.

"What's wrong, Father?" I asked.

"I like to be outdoors when I think," he said. "I used to have my best thoughts when I was cultivating onions, back before you were born."

"What about now?" I said. I knew how to think: I thought of things to do, places to venture on the Bidwell System; I had problems to solve in cyberschool.

"I think," he said. "But I am not thoughtful. Out here, thoughts grow. They are vertical and not horizontal." He held his arms up to me. "Come," he said, "sit in my lap."

I was not used to being held by my father, but I did as he asked. He put his arms around me as though I were the onion and he the earth. He smelled deep and rich with a smell I hadn't experienced for a long time. I shut my eyes and thought of what it would be like to stay in his lap, protected and warm, nothing to do but grow.

"Among the onions," he said, "it was quiet, and sure. Rooted."

My mother came to the door. "Your helmets are beeping," she said. Project Bidwell, the directors had reminded us again and again, would not work were we to slip away from our helmets for long periods of time.

But we could slip off, *into* the computer anytime we wanted, and I did. At first, for fun, I would run away into cyberspace, seeing how far I could travel into the virtual world before my parents found me. Most of the time, I spent hours making virtual friends at cyberschool (it didn't matter when I clicked into that part of the program, though I learned the habits of some of the other children in Bidwell). You see, I was an only child. The son of an only child. I could have created a cyberbrother, I know, maybe an older one who could show me the way into things, someone I could imitate; or maybe a younger one, someone to boss around, to try to leave behind, stuck on some old key system like a computer before there were mouses. I could have created more pets, too, or found cyberpals all over the world.

Instead, our small family stayed close together – I sat between my mother, with her ambition for the future, and my father, with his struggle to keep up with her. Although our small domed unit was, at times, claustrophobic – three computers in comfortable chairs downstairs, along with one bathroom, and three beds upstairs   nobody lived in a broader world, no body could go more places, see more things, learn more quickly than we could. "We live in the mind," my mother said over and over. "Most of life is spent in the mind, anyway, isn't it?"

"An onion is outside the mind," said my father. "It needs care."

"What did Father mean about an onion and care?" I asked my mother later.

"He misses some of his old world," explained my mother. "Don't worry about him. Peel a cyberonion and see what is there."

I did, and watched layer after layer come off until, on the very inside, there was no inside. It was all layers after all.

"You see," said my mother, "an onion, cyber or grown in the earth, is perhaps no more real than a computer system. Layers and layers of programming create this nonpolluting, resource-saving world. No matter what's inside, it's the layers that are important."

"A cyberonion," said my father, "is not a real onion." He liked to call one up, peel it, try to enjoy its cybersmell and cybertaste. "A real onion can make you cry."

"How can an onion make somebody cry?" I asked my mother.

"Chemical reaction," she said.

"But it takes a real onion," said my father. "And a real somebody."

My father had, he told me, a worker's body, a body that liked to bend to the earth, to dig, to hoe, to pause for a moment and look around, smelling whatever might be on an afternoon breeze, predict the weather. In Bidwell, however, we floated in cyberspace hour after hour, our minds doing everything – even touching and eating, smelling and tasting – all with no stimulus but the simulations made of dots and our memories. Floating, my father did not tire, and as mother and I slept, readying ourselves for a new cyberday, my father lay awake, his body remembering the long hours with his physical self that had once brought him a need for rest and sleep.

In those long nights when there was little to do, Father had time to think. Often, he lay staring at his collection of onions that had grown oddly in the ground. He had carried his jars everywhere with him; they were the only things he refused to have scanned into the Bidwell computer. The government had permitted him to keep his collection in our small dome. These pickled onions were my father's constant reminder of his other world. With them, he remembered how, as a young man, he had become intimate with the nature of the earth and onions. How, when he and mother first married, the smell of onions was on his hands. He remembered the soreness of a body saturated with work, the satisfying thud of an onion tossed gently into a box, the sharp taste of the raw yellow onion, the sweet purple of the red onion, the crispness of a white onion, its skin flaking like snow. He missed onions.

And the more he stared at his collection, the more they became fixed, permanent, never changing: like cyberonions. Of course they looked different than their computerized counterparts: in some of the jars were onions with double, triple, even quadruple bulbs – huge things the size of babies' heads; in one jar was an onion with indentations that made it replicate exactly the profile of George Washington; another onion had grown around a small rock so that it looked like an innertube floating in its juice; still another reached up with two stems, like the arms of a man reaching to the sky, asking for rain.

In those long nights, my father grew to hate even these odd onions, for they reminded him that he no longer had the chance to grow other, stranger, more exotic ones. My father became, during his long nights awake staring at deformed onions, dissatisfied not only with the quality of the cyberonion, but with the cyberworld itself.

My mother tried hard to console him. Then she made a suggestion: my father and I might seek the permission of the Project Bidwell officials to create a better onion, to perfect the cybersmell and cybertaste, to match Bidwell onions to the real sensations my father knew so well. With his memory and my computer skills, we might even be allowed to attempt the creation of odd onions, nonuniform, since the ultimate goal of the cyberworld programmers was to learn to mimic the randomness of the genetic world.

My mother, one of the most enthusiastic of those early Bidwellians, made the plea to the officials for this personal project. "This is the same man who married me in a chat room, who has followed me into cyberspace, who, though a reluctant pioneer, a hesitant astronaut, will help us move forward, into the beyond that beckons past Bidwell."

And they, loving such rhetoric, granted their permission.

Upon hearing the news, I clicked into the Bidwell Workshop, where the project officials had secured all the tools: from the graphics to stimulate the eye to the impulses that would be delivered to the helmet to make the brain experience taste, texture, smell.

"No," said my father. He took off my helmet and led me to his jars of pickled onions. "First we will study this thing, the onion. I will tell you what I know of it."

My father described onions to me in all their forms. He even wanted me to know of rotting onions, with their distinct pungency and their bruised flesh. He recalled to me the odd molds that lived in onions, folding them-selves between layers like sprinkles of pepper. He remembered how the brown, yellow, and white skins flaked from the onion and littered the kitchen of the farmhouse where he'd grown up. He wanted the same thing to happen in the kitchens of cyberspace. He praised the beauty of the striped effect of a red onion when it was sliced lengthwise. We would, he said, try to re-create it. And the roots: none of the cyberonions I'd seen had roots, which he told me were once-live, once-soft tendrils that always found what the onion needed, and yet, when dry, seemed insubstantial, coarse, as ephem-eral as the beard on a goat. He described how the top of an onion might bolt toward its flower, how the stiffest shoot thrusts out of the plant, stops sud-denly, and grows from its tip the soft green tendrils, like coarse hairs, each one with a tiny white flower, the flowers together shaped like a small onion, with a deeper smell of onion and earth, like no other smell in all the world, or cyberworld.

You must remember that I am amplifying my father's lessons concerning the onion. I try to allow for his emotion, his enthusiasm. His exact words, if I recall, were something like: "A green shoot, see, and little flowers, bunched up in a ball. Good smell – like soil, like onion. I wish you could smell it." You see, my father's memory of onions far exceeded his ability to describe them, just as my mother's ambitions for us in cyberspace far outpaced her ability to make us understand just what she envisioned for our future.

Our future, at least for long days and nights in our small, dome-shaped domicile, became the onion: the long attempt to re-create the onion began. We started, of course, with the program the Bidwellians had written to cre-ate the cyberonion. After I examined it, I saw how simple it was, like a child trying to draw the world with a box of six Crayolas. In fact, I began to won-der if all of the cyberworld I'd grown so used to was equally simple.

"What's in the program to create the *texture* of the onion?" asked my fa-ther.

"The same coding they've used for the apple." I did more research. "And the potato." I visited the programming for other vegetables. "And the carrot, only without as much bite factor."

"Can we use any of it, or shall we start over?" he asked.

I went to my mother. "Remember," she said, "everything is layers. It's like a chemical formula. Many things are made of carbon, hydrogen, and oxygen, the simplest building blocks. The *way* they come together can make the simple very complex. Start where they've started and make a complex onion."

I tried to do as my mother suggested. I tried everything out on my father. He tried everything out on his memory of onions. Each time, I failed.

"Make it fun," said my mother.

"Are you sure they're giving you access to everything?" asked my father.

For weeks and weeks I tried my limited programming abilities. I consulted with others, I examined my father's pickled onions until they haunted my dreams and my waking, I bounced between my mother's exhortations to try and my father's frustration at our failure.

And then, one day, like a cyberthief, like what in the very old days the authorities called a "hacker," I suddenly found my way onto a screen I had never seen before, in a territory layered inside Bidwell, layered below the Bidwell Workshop, and layered even inside the tools they had given me. I was as close to the center of cyberspace as I'd ever been. And what I saw helped me to understand why I could not create an onion with my limited tools: I, myself, was being limited.

You see, I was staring at the same programming that controlled the helmet I wore, and my father's helmet, and my mother's, too. I might have been a child in the days before the cyberworld, looking at a picture of his skeleton on X-ray film.

And when I saw my program, I had a thought I should never have had. I thought that maybe, just maybe, I wasn't real at all, but a cyberperson, like my dog, Sunflower, was now a cyberdog. Had my parents, I wondered, scanned me into the computer, too, as part of the resource-saving, energy-reducing, space-limited cyberworld? Was the skeleton on the X-ray film only a picture of a child?

I must have screamed, for suddenly my mother and my father tore off their helmets and surrounded me with their concern. I was too upset to explain what I had come to question. But, somehow, my father understood. Perhaps he was equipped to know my fear best.

He went to his collection of onions, those jars of actual onions in actual vinegar. His eyes gleamed as he shattered a jar against the wall.

"Do you smell that?" he shouted. He reached down for an onion and rubbed it against his pants leg.

"Feel," he commanded. He grabbed my hand and put it on the onion skin. Evaporating vinegar cooled my fingers.

He took a large, crunching bite of the onion. "Taste," he said. He tore off a nibble and put it into my mouth.

I cannot describe this experience, just as my father could not describe *his* knowledge of onions to me. It was, as I learned later, an experience like faith: something happens, something is there, but how can anyone prove its existence?

"You see," said my father. "If they cannot make a decent cyberonion, and now you know they cannot, then they cannot make a cyberboy who could taste a real onion and know the difference."

He began picking up the onions that had rolled into odd places around the room. "You are mine," said my father. "And your mother's. You live in Bidwell, but you are not Bidwellian."

And then he reached into his pants pocket and pulled out a small packet. He tore an edge from it and shook some small black grains – they looked like crushed pepper – into his hand.

"Your mother says life is but layer after layer, created by memory or by a computer – what is the difference? The Bidwellians want you to believe so, too."

He took me outside to where he used to sit on the ground. He scratched the surface of the earth. "*This* is different," he said, and he took a small black seed, bent down, and pushed it gently into the exposed soil.

"Should you try to remove the layers, you would destroy the life that waits inside here, the life that makes you, and me, and computers, and all of Bidwell." He covered up the seed and gently stepped on the ground.

My mother watched from the doorway. She didn't say a word when our computer helmets began to beep. But my father started back into our small home. I stared after him.

"Father, wait," I said. "How can we leave this place?"

He turned to me and laughed. "Because it is *not* cyberspace. Because it will always be here. Because this onion seed will grow into an onion, programmed by nothing more than the earth itself. Onion to seed to onion to seed."

And so we went back to Bidwell, donned our helmets, and logged into cyberspace, a place no *more* real, though increasingly no *less* real, than the small patch of scratched earth outside the door of our small, domed shelter. We, like so many of our human counterparts, learned to live in both worlds: to dream and to wake, to learn and to imagine, to live between two lives, almost like a boy might sit between a mother and a father, learning to grow, and to grow onions.

And that, I conclude, represents the complete and final triumph of the onion, at least as far as my family is concerned.

The Summer Grandma Was Supposed to Die

The summer Grandma was supposed to die, we headed west from Topeka most every Saturday or Sunday to what my mother called the "home place." My father stayed home. "He deserves his weekends," Mom said.

I remember one Sunday in particular, in what must have been August. Early in the morning I was awakened by my parents' bitter voices. Over cereal, Mom gave us boys her look that said, "Get ready." My father was still in their bedroom, shades pulled to make it dark.

My brother and I moaned. "Why do we have to go?" I asked. "I hate it in the car. It's boring. There's nothing to see and there's nothing to do."

"There's everything to see, Ellis," said my mother. "You just have to know where to look. And your grandmother won't always be here."

"She's not here," I said. "She's there. She's very far away."

"Well, you ought to be glad she's there. Remember, that's where I grew up. You'll care about that some day."

"I don't care about anything," said my little brother, Trego. "I don't care if Grandma dies. I wish she would die."

Mother sighed. "You boys be in the car in ten minutes. And not another word."

We rode in our red Plymouth station wagon, our heads and arms leaning out the windows: 1962 was before we had automobile air conditioning. I tried to see whatever my mother said there was to see. The land changed mile after mile: its flesh fell away, it began to bald, it dried from heat that increased the farther west we went. In the five hours it took to reach Ogallah, the land turned into a skeleton, as white and parched with dust as the cattle skulls we found when Mom and Grandma turned us loose to explore the pastures our grandmother leased to the local ranchers.

Trego provided the entertainment. One of his last baby teeth was loose, and he pressured it with his tongue and pried it with his fingers until it streaked with blood. Finally, in an act of daring born of boredom, he asked for a napkin and yanked the tooth out. The bloody stump was impressive. The empty cavity leaked until the napkin turned completely red. "I'm keeping this tooth forever," said Trego. He grinned, and all of his mouth was red, the blood staining his teeth like small veins.

"Close your mouth. You look hideous," said my mother, but that only kept him going.

His mouth had stopped bleeding by the time we reached the home place, seven miles north of Ogallah. Grandmother waited for us in her chair in the kitchen. There was always food: "Generous neighbors," she always said, though I'd never met them. I wondered if the neighbors were the men in dust-choked pickups who lifted a single finger off the steering wheel to greet us as we passed them on the gravel roads that chewed the underside of our station wagon.

We ate, Trego favoring one side of his mouth. My mother brought him a small cup, and he put his stumpy little tooth in water to soak: it was a miniature version of Grandma's dentures, which often sat dead at the bottom of yellowing water in her bedroom, a place of crumpled sheets and strewn clothing and ugly smells.

After food, after cold water pumped up from the well, bitter with minerals, Grandma told us boys: "You go on now, find yourselves something to do."

"You're responsible for Trego," Mom reminded me as we ran out into the western Kansas summer of dry heat delivered by a wind constantly alive, forceful, pleading with everything to do something. We usually had only an hour or so before Mom stood in the driveway honking the horn to round us up for the interminable trip home.

I was twelve, Trego was ten. We were happy to be out of the dusty house where mother sat with Grandma, the curtains drawn to keep the sun from making each room a small furnace. In the still kitchen, they spoke quietly, as though at a funeral instead of just visiting. We never knew what they found to talk about.

"Grandma's diseases," said Trego.

"No," I said, "probably about inheritance and stuff." My brother didn't know what inheritance was, so he stayed quiet.

"Ellis?" he asked. "Do you remember Grandpa?"

"He had a long white beard," I said. "I touched it at the funeral. I thought he was going to bite me."

"I wish I was home with Dad," said Trego.

"Dad doesn't want you home with him," I said. He didn't want any of us home, I thought. "Let's go to the sand slide," I said, and began to run.

A hundred years before, a branch of the Saline River had run near the house, and the soil was half sand climbing up to higher ground. We could jump down what used to be the riverbank and slide twenty feet without stopping. Trego ran after me, but I was first to the top, and then quickly to the bottom. The gritty sand worked its way into my shoes. Soon it would fill my pockets, even find its way into my underpants enough to make the ride home uncomfortable. But I didn't care. I hollered my pleasure, and Trego followed me down.

He slid directly into my back. His stupid shoes clobbered me hard. "Damn you!" I yelled. I outweighed him by twenty pounds, and I reached around, grabbed him by the shoulders, and let that weight drag him to me, then over me. I let go, and he somersaulted to the bottom of the little hill. He lay flat on his back, his breath coming hard, his face crusted up with tears. I sat above him, waiting for him to move. I wasn't mad at Trego. I was king of the mountain. King of the riverbank. King of all I could see, which in that landscape went for miles and miles, vision lost only in the haze of forever. I remembered what my mother said about seeing.

That's when I heard the snake. Grandma and Mother were always warning us of prairie rattlers, but I'd never seen one. This time, I saw the snake, brown like the dusty sand, coiled into a ring, head mounted, tail erect and shaking, making a sound not so much like a rattle as like a stuttering hiss of wind in a hollow rock. The rattler was three feet from Trego. Before I could think what to do, it struck at him, at his leg.

Trego sat up and yelled, then crab-walked backwards, toward me. For a terrible second, the rattler held on. I prayed for it to die, like a bee after it delivers its worst. And then, probably losing its grip on my brother's flesh, and finding itself with only a mouthful of denim, the snake let loose. Both of us ran up the old riverbank, this time watching all around us, seeing danger behind every rock, in every clump of yucca, even lurking in the smooth wire of buffalo grass on the bank's edge. The snake did not follow us: we watched it slither across the sand.

"Let's see," I said. Trego lifted his pants leg. Two tiny rivulets of blood, like tears, ran from his leg into his sock. "Are you okay?" I asked.

Trego didn't answer. He looked at me, his face as pale as the dry midday sky, and then he fainted.

We were a quarter mile from the house. I lifted Trego in my arms and I walked. The same body I'd so easily flipped over me was a huge sack of sand. The same dusty ground I'd run over so easily now sucked me down like quicksand. The same house we'd run from so eagerly for distance would not come closer. My mouth dried out, and with each step I worried that I, too, might hear the rattle, feel the sharp sting of the prairie.

Instead, leg-weary, arm-cramped, dry-mouthed, panting, I made it to Grandma's porch and banged unmercifully on the screen door. Mom came out with her best scolding expression, then screamed. "A snake," I said. "A snake bit him on the leg. A rattlesnake."

"Mom!" yelled my mother. "Mom! Trego's been snake-bit. Mom! Where's the kit, Mom!"

All that summer, I had not once seen my grandmother move from her chair. Suddenly, she was on the porch. She kneeled abruptly next to Trego, a small knife in one hand, a dishcloth in the other. She wrapped the cloth around Trego's knee and knotted it so hard her old knuckles cracked. She sliced his pant leg to expose the bite, then she made two quick incisions in his leg. She bent over him and began to suck on his leg. "Oh, God. Oh, God," said my mother over and over.

Grandmother came up for breath and spit a mouthful of blood onto the ground. Then she bent to her work, sucking and spitting again and again. I watched, helpless, while my mother went for Mercurochrome and gauze, then to start the car. My grandmother finally paused. She looked at me and smiled, toothless, her gums stained with Trego's blood, as though someone had just pulled all her teeth out of her mouth. "You did right, Ellis," she said. "Thank goodness you're a strong boy."

I began to cry. My mother carried Trego to the car. Grandma sat next to him in the backseat. I sat next to Mom in front. At the hospital in WaKeeney an old doctor gave Trego a shot. He was wide awake by then, and he jumped with the pain. "He'll be fine, Eleanor," the old man said to my grandmother. She held her hand over her mouth to cover her smile, probably embarrassed because her teeth weren't in. As we left her on her porch, Grandmother said to my mother, "You do what you have to do. That's life." Trego slept all the way home.

That was our last trip to western Kansas that summer. Grandma didn't die, not for another five years, when I was seventeen. By then, I loved the "home place." Trego did, too. My father and mother made peace between them, and they both took us boys to Ogallah about once a month. When Grandmother died in the late spring of 1967, we loaded up the car for the last time. Western Kansas was all green with winter wheat and buffalo grass. The chalk bluffs, the skeleton of that land, lay bleached and exposed. The sky was a cloudless blue. In the car, I punched Trego in the arm. "Whatever happened to that tooth you lost?" I asked.

"Lost," he said. "I don't care. Another one grew in."

My grandmother had her false teeth in for her funeral. But as I bent over her, I thought of her toothless mouth, full of blood. I thought of her quiet strength, of all that she knew or had known. I thought of the land, how each time I might see it for the first time, if I knew where to look, how to look. Luckily, it would always be there.

Shopping

Even though the supermarket is laid out so shoppers go from bakery to produce to meats, then to dairy, then to aisle after aisle of packaged and canned goods, Sam Mitchell insists on pushing an empty cart to the back of the store. His son, Conrad, always says the same thing, "Can't you just fill it up as you go?"

"Your mother shopped like this. 'Backwards,' she said. 'You like your bread crushed by kidney beans?' she used to ask. 'Your lettuce wilted by ice cream?' She knew what she was doing."

"You're not supposed to eat ice cream," Conrad says.

"I don't," says his father.

"You buy it every week," Conrad says.

"Company," says his father, and gives the cart a sudden push.

Conrad catches up to him. "I'm just telling you what your doctor told me."

"You drive me to the store," says his father. "Do I ask you to come in?"

"I drive you to the doctor's, too," says Conrad, "and *he* wants me to come in."

"So I'm the only one who needs to worry about my health?"

But Conrad has no symptoms of anything except grief: a dead mother, an aging father, a lover who moves in and out of illness like Conrad moves in and out of hope.

Sam pushes his empty cart forward. They might as well be strangers who happened into the store at the same time: one in his seventies, big, almost overweight, leaning heavily into the cart, his scuffed shoes barely lifting off the floor with each step; the other in his forties, in running shoes, no cart or basket, who might have popped in for one quick item and then hurried back to a busy schedule.

But the doctor has put Sam on a diet, and when he shops by himself, he brings home junk food – all chocolate chip cookies and no bread. Or two pounds of bacon and no fruit. Or something Conrad's mother used to prepare for him – say, a three-pound corned beef – which Sam has no idea how to cook in the mini-kitchen of Hillview.

By this time, Sam has made his way across the supermarket to the shampoo, the aspirin, the toothpaste.

"You don't need any of this stuff," Conrad says. "We bought razor blades last week."

But his father will travel every inch of the store, pushing his wobbling cart as though it were a walker. "Saw a commercial for that Dimetapp." His father is a head taller than Conrad, so that when he talks, his tendency to stoop matches Conrad's tendency to raise himself up on his toes.

"Do you have a cold?" asks Conrad.

"If I did, I'd buy Dimetapp." His father narrows his eyes. "Whew, they don't tell you the price on TV, do they?" He studies the medicines as though in need of whatever might cure him. "Tylenol reacts with alcohol," his father says. "To ruin your liver. A college girl died somewhere."

Conrad says nothing.

"Who can trust medicines these days," says his father. He pushes the cart down the aisle. "You're losing your hair," he says. "I can see the light reflecting off your scalp."

They pass by the vitamins. "You haven't bought One-A-Days for the longest time," says Conrad. He reaches for a package with the word SILVER on it.

"I don't believe in vitamins," his father says.

"Your doctor . . ."

"Doctors work for these people," says his father. "You want to pay a kickback, put those vitamins in here. You ought to know something about doctors by now."

Conrad tosses the vitamins in the cart and they move toward the dairy section, beer to the left, eggs to the right. When his father grabs a carton of eggs, Conrad asks, "Should you eat a dozen eggs every week?"

"Each egg has more vitamins than one of those god-awful pills in that vitamin bottle."

Sam reaches for the butter, ignoring margarine and elevated cholesterol. If Conrad suggests margarine, he hears, "I grew up on butter, and look how I grew," or "We used to have to squeeze the yellow into that white gunk that looked like lard," or "Butter is butter, but read the list of what they put in a tub of margarine."

When Conrad used to shop with Bill, he would sometimes imitate his father, the two men laughing, disapproving each other's choices. "Sour cream is sour cream," Conrad might say. And Bill, "Sour puss is sour puss."

Sam proceeds through the dairy section. Milk, whole. Presliced American cheese. Cream cheese. He stops near a bin of plastic-encased cheese and crackers, complete with a flat red stick for spreading the cheese. "One nice thing about getting old," he tells Conrad. "You don't really eat. You snack."

"What's your refrigerator like today?" Conrad asks. "Will you have room for anything?"

"I can't see *in*to the damn thing," says his father. "They put it down low, as though all of us were the size of women."

Conrad takes the same deep breath he's forced to take before he cleans his father's apartment-size refrigerator each week.

"Why do you *do* this," he asked the week before, pointing to a kitchen counter loaded with all he'd recovered from the tiny refrigerator: all that smelled, that grew mold, that was coagulated, or runny, or dry as brick.

"Nothing tastes like it should a second time," his father said.

"Then throw it away," Conrad almost screamed.

"Your mother loved leftovers," said his father.

"My mother is dead," Conrad said flatly.

"Not to me," his father answered.

Conrad sighs. They need nothing more in dairy.

"They probably *do* build those retirement apartments with women in mind, since women tend to live longer than men," says Conrad.

"Don't talk to me about long life," says his father. He pushes forward, down that odd aisle of motor oil, light bulbs, soda.

And pet supplies. "You remember Frankie?" his father asks.

"She scared me," says Conrad.

"She was already old when you were born," says Sam. "Your mother wanted a dog named Frank, after one she'd had when she was a child. But she fell in love with a female, so it was Frankie. She was the queen when you were born. Didn't like you at first."

"Who didn't like me? Mother or Frankie?"

His father turns to him as though hurt. "I wonder at your sense of humor."

"I followed Frankie next door one day," says Conrad. "When the Duncans were there. They had a little Chihuahua, with pups. Kept them in the garage. I was looking at the pups – I don't know where the mother was – when Frankie went after them. Pulled one of them out of the box and dragged it across the cement."

"Wanted to be a mother again," says his father.

"She killed the puppy. Don't you remember how mad the Duncans got?"

"I find that hard to believe," says his father.

"I saw her," says Conrad. "She broke that puppy's neck."

"Frankie died of a cancer," says his father. "Just like your mother. Do you remember the lumps?" He turns the corner into the next aisle: cleaning supplies, detergents, mops, brooms, sponges, bleaches, dishwashing soaps.

"I don't," says Conrad. "I was away. At college."

The two men walk silently, neither reaching for anything.

Conrad cleans his father's apartment every other week, if he can. Bill used to help him. Sam insisted that both of them wear latex gloves. His father tried to make it a joke. "The house surgeons," he called them.

Once, when his father was in his bedroom and Conrad and Bill in the kitchen, Bill took off his thin glove and blew into it until the fingers inflated into a balloon hand. "Mickey Mouse," Bill joked, "prepared to deal with all the assholes in the world."

"Don't be goofy," Conrad joked.

"Mickey had his Minnie. Donald had his Daisy. But what about Walt Disney?" Already, Bill's inflated hand was limp. "I'm melting, I'm melting," he said.

Sam poked his head out of his bedroom. "Once, when I was in Kansas City," he said, "I was just a young man, walking around, and all of a sudden I looked up at this door . . . it was a rundown building . . . and on this wavery glass, in flaky letters, was 'Walt Disney.' He got his start in Kansas City."

Bill put his latex glove back on his hand, which looked as wrinkled as Sam's face. "I'll research that," said Bill. He and Conrad went back to their cleaning.

His father hates cereals but loves to examine that aisle. "The bright boxes of nothing," he says, as he says every week. "Your generation was the first to really fall in love with sugar-coated grain."

"So *that's* where we went wrong."

"Fruit Loops," his father reads from a box.

"That's what we called those little loops of material they sewed onto shirts, in the back, on each side of the center pleats. Remember when everyone had to have those?"

"What nonsense."

"You have one on your shirt today," Conrad reminds him.

"That's not my fault," says his father. "Your mother picked out this shirt."

"She had style. She knew clothes. She had an eye, like Bill."

"She had style, but she wasn't *all* style."

"Neither is Bill," says Conrad. "Don't be rude just because you don't like him."

"Do you expect me to like him?" They are in the aisle of coffees and teas. Sam parks the cart near the Folgers but points to bag after foil bag, reading, "Macadamia Nut Decaf, Irish Vanilla Creme, Swiss Mocha Almond, Mocha Mint Almond Decaf. Why can't coffee just be coffee?"

"Have you tried any of those?" asks Conrad.

"Why would I?" His father puts a pound of Folgers in the cart, and Conrad hopes he'll be spared the lecture on how, these days, a pound of coffee costs more while the can contains only thirteen ounces.

Conrad moves ahead, past the canned soups and meats – the tuna, baby shrimp, Hormel chili, and Spaghetti-O's – turning the corner into the long aisle of frozen foods. He doesn't wait for his father to follow him, doesn't stop until he's halfway down the bright, cool length of the aisle, next to the bin full of frozen juices. He reads the labels, with their variety and combinations of strawberry, mango, grapefruit, kiwi, passion fruit, lime, orange, red raspberry. He wonders if someday he might feel the same intense disapproval as his father. He can hear his father's voice: "People think they need something new every single day."

Sam catches up to Conrad with a cart increased by half a dozen Campbell's soup cans. Conrad says what he says every week: "Did you check the sodium? Why not get the low-salt ones?"

"I've bought low salt," says his father. "You know what I do?"

Conrad knows.

"I put salt in them at the table." His father adds a small can of orange juice concentrate to his cart. The freezer cases on the opposite wall are full of frozen dinners: Weight Watchers, Healthy Choice, Stouffer's Lean Cuisine. He pushes away, saying, "I remember when we used to buy food because it *contained* calories."

The chips aisle used to be difficult, but his father has settled into a routine of one bag of fat-free pretzels a week, his only easy concession to the doctor's concerns. Often, he is eating the last pretzel as Conrad picks him up for the shopping trip.

First, Sam nibbles off the nubby ends where the dough laps out of the circles. Then he bites out the tops of what looks like two conjoined hearts, turning them into a W. If he's lucky, he'll be able to eat out the center of the W and make it a U, a kind of wishbone shape that he breaks in two, eating the bigger piece first, then the smaller. Conrad hates to watch.

Once, Bill bought Sam a package of thick pretzels, salt free, with some kind of mustard glaze. They sat in his father's kitchen for a month, unopened. "Aren't you going to at least try them?" Conrad asked before a shopping trip.

"Tell Bill to be his own guinea pig," said his father.

"I won't tell him anything," said Conrad. "He's got enough on his mind."

Conrad ripped open the bag and bit off one of the nubby ends. The glaze was sulfurous, the dough bitter. Conrad could hardly chew. He crushed the bag into the trash.

Even though Sam has quit buying bottled juices and is forbidden chocolate chip cookies, he turns his cart down that aisle as he does every other. Conrad walks ahead, hoping to speed his father's journey through the store. "Your mother always knew what was in the store," says his father. "Even the things she didn't buy."

Conrad turns to his father. Nobody else is in the aisle. "She was always very patient," he says.

"Right," says his father. "She lived with me."

"And with me," says Conrad.

"You weren't hard to live with until after her death," says his father. "Until after Bill."

"She knew about Bill," says Conrad. "About Bill and me."

"She didn't need to know. She had enough to worry about at the end. She couldn't even eat, just little swallows of melted ice cream. And *you* had to tell her about Bill."

"I wasn't telling her about Bill, I was telling her about myself."

"What's the difference?" says his father, and pushes his cart forcefully around the corner. He just misses a pyramid of on-sale pork and beans. He intensifies his shopping, pulling cans of his favorite vegetables off the shelves even though his cabinets are full of unopened cans.

Conrad wonders why he shops with his father at all. Of course the man would buy all kinds of artery-plugging, blood-pressure-raising, bowel-impacting food. But maybe they'd both be happier. His father could disobey doctor's orders without the constant conflict. And Conrad has enough to worry about with keeping Bill on doctor's orders.

The next aisle is called Rice and Ethnic. Besides produce, Conrad likes this part of the store best, especially since the grocer has brought in exotic items: basmati rice, orzo, posole. Conrad sees a good price on some Minnesota wild rice and picks up the package. "Mouse turds," says his father.

Conrad decides to remain silent for the rest of the trip. Let his father buy whatever the hell he wants. *Not* buy the grains he should have for fiber. Let the old man ruin his health. Let him die if he wants to.

Conrad puts the package of wild rice back on the shelf and almost jogs into the next aisle: spices, sugar, flour, and all the boxes promising quick and delicious breads, cakes, and muffins. He imagines his father following him, loading his cart with chocolate chips, sugar, Crisco. He wonders how his own health has remained intact, given his mother's cancer, his father's tendency toward high blood pressure, borderline diabetes. Around Bill, he feels guilty. His energy, his endurance, his muscle tone, his lack of symptoms, all seem to mock Bill. Maybe they mock his father, too.

Conrad passes the school and stationery supplies. Everything is more brightly colored, more interesting than when he was in school. Conrad remembers childhood as a kind of torture, being a child as being lost. One year, he refused to go to school altogether. His father took off from work for

45

two days and, holding Conrad's third-grade hand, walked his son to school. Conrad can still see his father sitting in one of the tiny school desks, his long legs stretched into the aisle so kids had to hurdle them to get to the blackboard. When Conrad realized his father would sit in school with him until he went on his own, he stopped throwing tantrums each morning. "Teacher said to tell you hello," he told his father.

"Mary had a great big lamb," said Conrad's mother.

Conrad liked his father there, but he was embarrassed, too.

Conrad nears the end of the stationery aisle and has to fight the temptation to turn around and wait for the shambling man his father has become. He turns the corner and finds himself alone in an aisle of oil, vinegar, peanut butter, jelly, pickles, salad dressing, mustard, and hot sauces. Condiments.

A voice, along with the sharp stab of a cart in his side, startles him. "I'm almost finished," says his father. "Didn't need anything in the last row, don't need anything here."

Conrad turns to look in his father's cart. He hasn't put anything more in it since Conrad walked away. "Don't you usually have a list?" asks Conrad.

His father taps his head. "Toilet paper, lettuce, a loaf of bread, and I'm finished." His father backs his cart and begins to turn toward the paper goods aisle.

Conrad imagines a funny film, with his father, as the star, suddenly revved up and running backwards through the store, putting everything he's slowly accumulated in his cart back on the shelves, returning the shopping cart and bowing himself out the door. Conrad is not in the movie – though if it's been filmed while they've been shopping, he knows the character he plays: the sidekick, the Harpo to his father's Groucho, the Lucy to his Desi, the Curly Joe to his Larry and Mo. Watching it in reverse would be the only thing that would keep it funny. Everything had been better when his mother was alive. The acting was better, the parts more tender and sophisticated, with more range and depth.

"Conrad," says his father.

Conrad is startled again by his father's voice. He moves toward him and leans an arm against one side of the grocery cart. He does not look at his father's face.

"Your mother ..."

"Bill visited Mom in the hospital. The week she died. He didn't even tell me he was going." Conrad focuses on the package of vitamins. "It was dark. After dinner. She had never even seen him before. But when he tapped on her door, and walked into the room, she whispered, 'Bill.'"

"Your mother ..." his father begins again.

"And she took his hand. And she tried to sit up like she always did when she had a visitor. But Bill sat down, so she didn't have to look up at him. So they were eye to eye." Conrad looks up at his father. "I can't tell you how many dying people Bill has visited."

"Your mother ..." his father says again, like an incantation.

"And do you know what she told him?" Conrad asks. "She told him to take care of me. Of *me*."

"Your mother," says his father, "was a better person than I am. She could worry about you without being angry." He is hunched forward, as though studying the food in his grocery cart. "Do I need to worry about you?" he asks.

"About my health?"

"Yes, of course."

"No. You can trust me about my health."

"Your mother was worried ..." says his father.

"About *you*," Conrad says. "She was worried about you." Conrad looks into his father's eyes. "I worry about you. Maybe I shouldn't."

"I hate shopping," says his father. "And going to the doctor. We always do the wrong things together."

"Mother wanted me to take care of you," says Conrad.

His father frowns. He shakes his big head. "So go get me toilet paper," he says. "That would be taking care of me."

Conrad is unsure of his father's tone. He starts away, then turns. "Get your own," he says. "Meet me at checkout. I'm going to buy some ice cream for Bill."

Conrad walks away for the second time during the shopping trip. He doesn't understand his father, but he is determined to wait as long as it takes – toilet paper, lettuce, and bread – for him to finish his shopping and arrive at the checkout counter.

47

Conrad goes to the freezer aisle. Just as his mother would do, he waits until the end of his shopping trip to buy the ice cream. He has to search, even open the freezer case to look behind other flavors of Ben and Jerry's, before he finally finds the last pint of Rainforest Crunch. When he makes it to the cashier, his father is not there.

Conrad waits patiently, looking over the headlines of the tabloids. Only his own life, he thinks, is more ridiculous. He will go from helping a grouchy and unappreciative old man do his grocery shopping to helping a sweet man do his dying.

The ice cream in his hand is so cold it hurts. Conrad breaks his resolve and starts through the store to find his father. He walks the aisles, glancing toward the racks of bread, the countertops full of fruits and vegetables. No father. Until there is only one place his father could be.

His father is just reaching for a card from the Hallmark section marked SYMPATHY. "I need ice cream, too," says his father. "Could you get me the same kind you have there?"

"This is the last one," says Conrad.

"Then get another kind. One that Bill likes. I want you to take it with you to the hospital today."

Conrad looks at his watch. "I need to hurry," he says.

"I'm ready," says his father. "I've found a sympathy card."

"For Bill? You mean a get well card?" Conrad looks for that section.

"Your mother hated get well cards. They just showed how people lie to each other. We don't have to lie about this, do we?" He puts his large hand on Conrad's shoulder.

"Meet you at the cashier." Conrad hurries back to the ice cream, picks out his father's favorite, mint chocolate chip. He has forgotten to put the Ben and Jerry's in his father's cart, and suddenly both hands are completely numb.

But then his father wheels up to the cashier. Conrad sees the place his father has made for the ice cream. "Not too close to the lettuce," his father reminds him. "Cold can wilt it."

Conrad puts the ice cream in the cart. And they stand in line, waiting to pay.

The Man Who Ran with Deer

Harry and Mavis marry late, just when they think marriage will never happen to them. And, just when they think they will never have a child, Mavis becomes pregnant. For three months, Mavis has terrible morning sickness. Harry is cautious of her moods, her sudden nausea, her new distance from him. She is a different creature. He wishes sometimes for their life before the pregnancy.

In the fourth month, Mavis finally feels better. She begins to show. Harry remains shy. He acts as though he has just met her. In the morning, he watches Mavis rise and put on her clothes. The slight swell of her womb embarrasses him. When she sees him looking, she hurries to the bathroom. Perhaps they are too old for the unexpected, Harry thinks. Too old for a child. Too worn, too much creatures of routine. He cannot talk. Mavis does not speak her feelings, either. They learn how easily quietness sets in.

Then, one morning, they sit like usual at the breakfast table. The first chores are done. Butter slowly melts into hot oatmeal. Scrambled eggs and coffee steam between them. Mavis looks out the window, across the draw, into the thirty-acre pasture rimmed by woods. They enjoy watching the dawn. This is their one time to relax, until evening, when the sun sets and they go to their bed.

Suddenly, Mavis jumps up out of her chair. "Harry," she says, "they've come back. But look." She points.

Harry looks. In the distance, where the pasture turns to trees, he sees the deer, a buck and two does, before he sees what looks like a man, naked, slightly stooped, moving among them. "What the heck," he says.

"It's a man," says Mavis. She crosses her arms over her chest and stares. "It's a man with them," she says again.

"What the heck," Harry says. He starts for the door.

"No," says Mavis. "You'll scare them away."

"I'll be quiet," Harry says, and leaves the house.

Outside, the sun rises into the woods, turning sky, trees, and pasture red, then bronze. Harry's cattle still nudge each other in the barn. Their one rooster decides to crow. Harry moves slowly across the graveled drive, through his waiting machinery, to the edge of the draw. He looks back at the house, expecting to see Mavis, but every window glares back at him with the reflection of the rising sun. When he looks back into the pasture, the deer and the man stand alert. They stare at Harry, then move, more gently than shadows, back into the woods. For a long moment, Harry watches the place where they disappeared. Then he goes back inside.

Breakfast is cold. "You frightened them away," says Mavis. "Who knows when they'll be back."

"That was a man with them," says Harry. "After breakfast I'm going to look for tracks."

Mavis says nothing, until, breakfast quickly eaten, Harry goes to the closet for his gun. "You don't hunt," says Mavis.

"Protection," Harry says. "If I see them, up close . . . If I get close to the man . . . If that man is crazy or something . . ." Harry doesn't know what he might do, but the gun makes him feel better.

"You've never shot a deer," says Mavis. "You've never shot a living thing."

Harry nods and walks out the door. He once killed a deer, when he was a young man, before he knew Mavis. When he married and took over the home place, he quit hunting. He lets her think what she thinks.

Harry climbs slowly through the draw up into the pasture and heads straight for the spot where he remembers seeing the man and the deer. By the time he reaches the edge of the woods, the sun is a brilliant yellow. Morning has separated the trees from their shadows. Although he sees the tracks of deer, Harry cannot find evidence of the man, either in the grass or in the soft earth around the oak and hickory trees. He wonders if he and Mavis really saw what they thought they saw.

He moves on into the woods, as silently as he can. After ten paces he realizes he is holding his breath. The air is still cool among the trees, and Harry walks until he reaches the barbed wire fence that separates his from his neighbor's property. He doubles back along the fence line, avoiding the few crisp early leaves, the few clumps of brittle grass, the few fallen twigs that might reveal his presence. He stops sometimes and stares hard in every direction, his head erect, his nose in the air.

After he walks the full half-mile through the line of timber to the road, seeing only what is familiar, Harry turns and starts back to the house. He cuts diagonally through ten acres of head-high corn, checking the ears. They are nicely formed, but he knows better than to call them money in the bank. By the time he is at the back of his barn, the August morning has declared itself as summer. He is sweating through his work shirt when he reaches the house.

"Nothing," he tells Mavis. "There's nothing out there." She is sitting at the table exactly where he left her.

"We saw them," she says. "We saw him with them."

"There's nothing there now," he says. "I didn't see a thing." He puts his gun in the closet. Still, Mavis does not move. She stares out the window. When Harry starts to clear away the dishes, she rises and starts her day.

For three days they watch and wait for what they might see. Harry does not mind the silence. Their mornings are a kind of meditation as they stare out across the pasture. The sun turns the tree leaves from black to silver to gold to green, their trunks from charcoal to fire to the color of upright earth.

Neither Harry nor Mavis can say exactly when the deer appear on the fourth day. One moment, the two of them sit, watching out the window. The next moment the deer are on the land, without movement, as though a shroud has been lifted from around them, as though something has lifted in Harry and Mavis. And before they exclaim at the sight, or at how their breaths both quicken before each one sighs, the man appears, too, slightly hunched, naked, hair the color of doeskin. The deer graze, the buck occasionally lifting his head erect to listen and smell, anticipating danger. The naked man stands very still, as calm as though he is asleep.

Harry pushes himself up from the table. Mavis puts her finger to her lips, as though any sound, even so far away as from their house, might scatter these animals into the woods. "I'm going," he says.

"Do you see him, too?" asks Mavis.

"Of course I see him," Harry says. "I'm going around the back way, behind the barn and around." He moves quickly to the closet, as though he can only make up his mind as he speaks.

"Not the gun," says Mavis. "You don't need it."

"Never know," says Harry as he leans in and grabs the gun from the corner.

Mavis does not look at him. She hasn't seen him since the deer appeared. She sits transfixed, instead, in her kitchen chair.

Harry leaves without looking back at her, or the house. He walks like his father taught him years before, the gun tucked loosely under his arm, its weight leaning against his forearm, the barrel pointing down. He has made sure the safety is on. He hurries through the barn, cuts across the cornfield, finds himself among brush and rock, then in the cool of the woods. He does not stop to look or listen until he judges himself to be a hundred yards from where the deer and the man were when he and Mavis saw them. He hopes they are still there.

As he nears the rim of the pasture, he is almost on tiptoe. The gentle sawing of crickets disguises the sound of his feet even from himself. He hears nothing but morning: a small throb of wakefulness, a low hum, as though someone is blowing a stream of breath into a huge jar. As he reaches an open space between trees, and finds his way into it to look toward dawn and deer, several birds scold him and fly away, hammering the air with their fright. When he looks where he wants to look, nothing is there.

He walks the edge of his pasture, anyway, stepping boldly now, until he reaches the spot where the deer and the man must have been. This time, he finds many signs: grass folded gently by the weight of large creatures; the ragged edges of nibbled brome; deer feces – small black pellets as round and distinct as marbles. He turns away to begin his walk straight back to the house and steps into another feces, brown, indistinct, as awkward as a stain. The smell reaches his nostrils at the same time as his realization that this is the sign of the man, and that it is very fresh, and that perhaps Mavis . . . He doesn't like to think about Mavis sitting at the breakfast table, watching this naked man do his business in the pasture. He scrapes his boot against clumps of grass and starts back to the house. Down in the draw he lets his foot wander into the creek. His boot is clean by the time he reaches home.

"You didn't even get close," Mavis says. "I saw you come out of the woods. They were long gone by then."

"I never could get close to deer," Harry says.

"He sure gets close to them," says Mavis. "They all just bounded off together. Even the man was beautiful to watch. Graceful when he moved. Like a dancer."

Harry looks at Mavis. Her voice sounds like it might if she were describing a dream: slightly distant, focused on the inside of her mind. He doesn't mention the dropping he has wiped and soaked off his boot. She doesn't mention it either. Behind on the day, they go off to their separate chores.

Late summer has its own rhythm of days, as dawn moves more slowly into the sky, as corn swells and stiffens in the fields, as brome reaches for a last cutting, as tree leaves gather an abundance of light and heat before fall. Harry and Mavis sit each morning watching for the deer, and the man.

For the first time in his life, Harry is intensely aware of things so small they have no names, and he has no way of talking about them with Mavis. They are things like the peculiar slant of light across an abandoned bird's nest so that the molted feathers glimmer like the lace trimming of a beautiful gown. Or the way sunset fills the barn with cracks of light so intense he feels like it might explode. Or his discovery of how each plot of earth, each plant, each piece of board, stone, and brick, is perforated, ready to rip away, separate, dissolve, given enough time.

Harry thinks constantly about the man who runs with the deer. Each morning he and Mavis watch through their breakfast, but Harry also watches through the rest of the day. At odd moments, he pauses from his work and stares in all directions, his nose in the air, his ears alert for any sound. He tells himself he is looking for the deer, and the man, but he feels like they are watching him, and he is trying to discover them doing it. As he moves through the daily work of the farm, he thinks of the creatures, and where they might be.

He and Mavis do not talk about it, except when the deer and man appear around breakfast, every week or so. Then Harry hurries out the door to see if he can get close. Sometimes he finds evidence: more human droppings;

once, a footprint, smaller than he expects, in the soft earth after a rain; another time a stripped ear of corn, thoroughly eaten to the cob in a way no raccoon would have the patience for.

Harry brings what news he can, though Mavis is not curious for his details. She is content to sight the deer, and the man, to watch them move out of, then back into, the woods, and disappear. As her womb swells, she seems to nest herself in her kitchen chair. Harry has quit taking his gun: he feels awkward with it resting in his arms.

One crisp morning on the edge of fall, Harry is out in the woods after he and Mavis have sighted the deer and the man. He traces a noiseless path toward the lip of the pasture where the man and deer have appeared. As he nears the open space where he wants to look out, he bends down and removes his boots. He wants the silence of human skin on earth. He edges forward, his feet stiffening with cold. He wonders again, as he has all through the cooling season, how the man keeps warm.

At the edge of the woods, Harry stations himself behind a hickory tree. He hugs its shaggy bark and leans his head around to see what he can see. For the first time, he is rewarded. There, fifty yards away, stand the buck, the two does, and the man. Harry has seen deer before, but never this close. He has seen naked men, too, but never this far away, never with deer, in his pasture. The man is slightly bent. His hair is shaggy. He has a tangled beard. He moves when the deer move; settles into his stoop when the deer graze the grass.

Harry watches quietly, not trying to move closer. He wonders if Mavis is watching for him, if she sees how close he has stalked them without frightening the animals away. The moment he has the thought, the deer move again, toward the woods. The man moves with them. Harry sees the white tail of the deer. The man has extraordinary body hair. Thick and brown, it cascades down his back, across his buttocks, and trails down his legs. The deer continue into the woods, slowly withdrawing, their movements fluid, full of grace. The man moves, too, slowly, raising his feet up and placing them down with the same cautious sureness, the same mincing elegance. As both man and deer disappear, Harry's toes, curled into the earth, begin to hurt. He lets go of the hickory tree. As quietly and gracefully as possible, he moves to the spot where he saw them last.

He sees them again. They are only a short distance into the woods, where another draw of the creek begins. A small spring trickles through limestone there, and gooseberries and pawpaws flourish. Harry hunches forward and tries to glide toward them between trees. For the first time, he is not hiding from them. He wants the man to see him. But what he sees makes him stop short, take refuge behind a cover of bushes. The man, thin and wiry as a hungry animal, approaches one of the does. He puts his arms up, toward her shoulders. He holds her against him. Though Harry cannot see well, he recognizes the act, has seen it many times among his cattle, horses, chickens, dogs, and cats. The man shudders, and moves away. The deer walk calmly down the draw, their hooves smushing in the soft earth, or sounding a hollow percussion against rock. Harry does not hear the man retreat. Harry does not try to follow them. He wishes for his boots, his kitchen, his breakfast, for Mavis.

When he returns, Mavis still sits by the window. "You got close this time," she says, not looking up. "I'll go with you next time."

"No," he says.

"I will," she insists.

"Well, I'm not going again," he says, but he doesn't tell her why.

When they don't see the deer or the man for over two weeks, Harry is relieved, Mavis disappointed. He feels haunted by the image of the man copulating with the beast. On the mornings he and Mavis speak at the breakfast table, he asks, "Why would a man want to run with deer?" or "Won't he quit soon, get someplace warm?" or "You haven't told the neighbors about him, have you?" Mavis doesn't answer. She is still fascinated. Harry hates to see her sitting there so eager to spot this naked man.

But it's worse when they finally see the creatures again, and Mavis stands up and puts on her brown jacket. She cannot zip it over the swell of her pregnancy. "Come on," she says.

"No," says Harry, "I've traipsed through the woods enough. Seen all I want to see."

"Okay," she says, "I've walked the place by myself before." She is out the door before Harry can argue with her, before he realizes he must go with her, that deer would never hurt her, but the man could, if he saw her alone. He goes to the closet for a jacket and his gun, then leaves the house, quietly. She'll be mad if he frightens the animals.

By the time he walks through the barn to the edge of the cornfield, Mavis is just disappearing into the edge of the woods. Harry feels odd, gun in hand, following Mavis without her knowledge, but he can't call out, or whistle. And then soon, he doesn't want to disturb the morning: a clear blue bowl of sky shot through with the last of the night's stars, a pale sliver of moon slowly disappearing in the gathering light, a delicate crunch of frost underfoot. Harry moves deliberately into his own frosted breath. The morning is so quiet Harry can stand still and hear Mavis walk, a hundred yards away, through the woods. She will frighten the deer and come home, he thinks. He follows after her.

He takes the cow path through the trees, moving, calmly and steadily, toward the places where Mavis has been. He can feel her lingering presence, as though they are in water and she has left a wake. Birds and insects begin to sound the morning air. Trees stretch into a rising morning breeze. Harry sees Mavis again, among some brush, at the edge of the pasture. Perhaps she is watching the deer and the man. Perhaps she is waiting for him. She stands very still, regarding the open space like a meditation.

Harry decides to get as close to Mavis as he can, without her seeing him. He leans his gun against a tree, takes off his boots, and continues toward her. It is all he can do to keep from shouting, bursting into laughter, clapping his hands. Hunched forward slightly, his breathing shallow and intense, his vision keen, his ears alert, he stalks his wife. From tree to hiding tree, he moves, pauses, moves again. He can think of nothing but coming upon her, maybe even reaching up to touch her, all without her knowing.

So he is surprised when, behind him, he hears movement, loud, awkward. He turns to see the deer, and behind them the man, drifting through the woods toward the fence line. Harry stands his full height to watch them disappear. Just before they do, the man who runs with the deer turns and looks back, his black eyes glistening as he moves a searching head. Harry cannot tell if the man sees anything but the backdrop of the woods he moves through.

Harry hears a sound. He sees the deer tense, then start away. The naked man shakes his head and follows. Harry looks toward the sound. Mavis is so close she can almost touch him. She smiles, then bursts out laughing. "I sneaked up on you," she says. "You didn't even see me coming."

Harry puts his finger to his lips. "Shhh, don't let him hear you. You don't know what he might do."

She is still smiling. "What could he do?" she asks. "He runs away, like the deer." Her voice is louder than he is used to, giddy, like it was when he courted her.

"He's not a deer," Harry insists.

Mavis looks at Harry, laughs at his stern face. "Where are your boots?" she asks. She puts toe to heel and kicks off one shoe, then the other. "Let's walk," she says, and takes his hand.

They move together toward the pasture, where the day has begun. When they see how bright it is on the grass, they stay on the pasture's edge, in shadow.

"Look," says Mavis, and she points to the house. Harry looks where she looks. The house shimmers with morning light; the drive circles it and snakes away toward town through a line of carefully planted trees; the garden beside it is still in neat rows, wilting tomato vines yielding up their last ripe tomatoes, as red as rising suns. The house is surrounded by machinery and buildings, everything that contains work and livelihood, everything that makes their life possible. Harry sees it all as though he is above it, with the knowledge of so many steps through the barnyard, so many times of turning the garden plot, so many years of riding the machinery, planting the trees, laying up wood, corn, hay, wheat. Harry and Mavis stand there looking, and Harry feels an uncommon joy. He imagines two people, sitting at the breakfast table, looking out, trying hard to spot deer. Instead, they see Harry and Mavis, just at the edge of the woods, holding hands.

Matty

We cleaned the house spotless: furniture dusted, floors vacuumed and mopped, bathrooms scrubbed. Then we started on ourselves, everything from behind the ears to clean toenails. Lined up for inspection in the kitchen, we gleamed like the Spic-and-Spanned floor, the Ajaxed sink. We piled into a car freshly waxed, recently vacuumed, the inside polished so that even the knob on the steering wheel glowed like a rare gem. Our mom and dad and little sister sat in the front seat of the old Hudson; we three boys sat in the back, the seat material as fuzzy and springy as our close-cropped hair. We breathed quietly, on edge because Mom and Dad were on edge.

"Well," said Dad when he backed the car out of the graveled drive. He aimed at the Union Pacific station across the Kansas River. Mom nodded, her face as solemn as an amen in the Episcopal church. We boys nodded like Mom, grinned at each other, but did not let our lips bubble into laughter.

We were on our way to meet Mom's Aunt Matilda. She was from New Jersey, a place we invoked with the mysterious words "Back East."

"Who *is* she?" we asked the week before. "Who is she to *us*?"

"She's my mother's cousin," Mom explained. "She's the daughter of my grandmother's sister. She's one of the few relatives left on my side. She's a librarian. Pay attention to her and you'll learn a few things."

Aunt Matilda's visit to Kansas meant everything to Mom, whose family was very small and very old, and, as she told us, formal and refined: ministers, teachers, librarians. They were people, we inferred somewhere in our eleven- and nine- and eight-year-old hearts, who might disapprove of our mom's early marriage ("Why, she's only twenty!") to a Kansan ("Why can't he stay in the East!"), and her move to the Midwest ("What do people *do* there but farm?"). They would see her immediate pregnancy ("They must have conceived on their wedding night!") and prolific family ("Can you imagine having *four* children?") as signs of poor taste, or lack of control. We had to pass Aunt Matilda's inspection, win her to our side, make sure she took only flattering remarks and positive stories to the few other aunts and uncles who would gather in a tearoom in the refined East for a firsthand report.

Our parents marched us into the Union Pacific station. We checked arrival times and headed to the track. We boys begged for coins. Dad found a penny, a nickel, and a dime. We didn't care who took which; by the time the train came and went, they would only be thin disks of copper, nickel, and silver.

Nothing beats waiting for a train. Anticipation hums like the tracks when the train is still miles away. The tracks themselves are so ordinary, steel bars, perfectly parallel, cold, and pinned to ties. Yet just touching a toe to one brings the greatest sensation of danger and fear, and makes a nervous mother scold with a tremendous scowl. We placed our coins and jumped behind the line Dad made with his foot. As we waited, people lined the tracks. The porters brought out their huge, metal-wheeled carts and stood at attention. And then the hum, and the deep chug, the shrilling whistle, the train itself looming up beside the river, rushing the station with a determination impossible to stop.

The engine towered in front of us, shot past as though it had forgotten Topeka altogether. Then: the sudden hiss of hydraulics, the fizz of steam and smoke released from between the cars, the shriek of steel on steel, the staring faces of those inside the passenger cars, the quick dismount of the conductors with their squat, four-legged stools, and, finally, passengers. We had seen her picture and heard Mom's warning: "Of course she's older now." But none of us recognized the short, pot-bellied woman who lugged a suitcase as unwieldy as she was. Her face was squat and puffed, with a protruding beak of a nose, recessed eyes, her head clamped by a feathered hat. Her legs were thin as sticks.

We waited too long in our places, until the woman set down her suitcase and searched the station platform. Mom approached, extended a white-gloved hand. "Aunt Matilda?" she asked, and when she found the hint of recognition, "I'm Mary. Welcome to Topeka."

"This is it, huh?" said Aunt Matilda. She looked at the old station, at the blue sky, at us. "I thought I'd never make it. I wouldn't let them take my bag from me." She winked at us children. "Too many goodies," she said. She smiled, and her teeth were as small as ours.

We kids broke apart; the tension of waiting patiently – for the whole week as well as at the station – sent us whirling around, slapping at each other. "Kids," said Dad, "you get back here, kids."

We were at the tracks, braving the steaming, hissing cars to find the coins we'd offered to the train. We brought them to where Mom stood talking about us. She said our names, and each of us held out a hand, palm up, to show the flattened coins.

"I'll trade you," said Aunt Matilda. "When we get home. A box of chocolates for those coins. Is it a deal?"

We nodded. "Can I get your bag, Aunt Matilda?" asked Dad.

"Matty," said Aunt Matilda.

"Matty," we said, trying something we had never called anyone before. "Matty, Matty, Matty."

"Boys," said our mom.

"What goodies are in your suitcase, Matty?" asked Beth. She was five.

"Well, you'll just see, little one," said Aunt Matilda, and she pressed down Beth's curls. They sprang back when she lifted her hand. Aunt Matilda readjusted the shoulder strap of a gigantic purse and we all followed Dad, who lugged the suitcase to the Hudson.

Dad stowed the luggage in the trunk. He and Mom and Beth climbed into the front seat while we boys, according to plan, squeezed into the back so that we left Aunt Matilda plenty of room. "Ouch," said Richard.

"Ouch yourself," said Robert.

"Ouch, ouch, ouch," we all repeated.

"Hush!" said Mom, shooting us a stern look. She had rehearsed us for Aunt Matilda's visit. We knew what we would eat for every meal, had even helped plan the menu so we wouldn't complain and ask questions every time we sat at the dining table. We knew who would sleep where, Richard giving up his bed to Aunt Matilda so that we three boys shared a room again, as we had when we were Beth's age. We knew what excursions we'd take, what hours to disappear so the adults could talk, what skills and talents we'd be expected to show off: Richard and his piano, Robert and his mighty baseball swing, Randall and his tumbling, Beth and what she called her dancing.

The entire week had the same regimen as a play. We had even pretended that Aunt Matilda was at the dining table, in the chair to the left of our dad. We practiced our manners: elbows off the table; left hand in lap as much as possible; small bites of food chewed all the way and swallowed before taking another; "please" and "thank you" and "you're welcome" used more liberally than sugar and salt; more food offered to others before seconds were taken for ourselves; main course finished by everyone before a mention of dessert; a polite "May I be excused, please?" once the entire plate was cleaned; plates cleared from the table when leaving.

We had the play in mind, but not always the proper attitude. So when Aunt Matilda dropped into the seat next to us, squeezing us even closer together, and Richard elbowed Robert trying to get more room, and Robert scooted Randall's knee against the door handle, and Randall raised his arm sharply, accidentally hammering Robert in the nose, and Robert turned quickly away, banging his ear against Richard's skull, we knew we should say "Excuse me" and "I'm sorry" and "That's all right," but we didn't. We shouted, we whined; tears popped out of our eyes. Dad turned around with his big arm and pinned down our legs.

"Sorry for the tight squeeze," said Mom, "but we didn't see the point in getting a sitter just for a trip to the station. Plus the kids all wanted to be the first to see you."

"I'm not squeezed," said Aunt Matilda.

We three boys huddled into the space of two seats to give her room. She filled her space, her purse on her lap. And she filled the back seat with an odd odor, a sharp smell like vinegar and perspiration and cats when they come in from the rain. For a proper lady from "Back East," she almost stank.

"How was your trip?" asked Mom.

"Long," said Aunt Matilda. "Who would have thought Kansas could be such a long ways from New Jersey."

"Halfway across the country," said Dad.

Aunt Matilda sighed. "Well," she said, "the longest trip is when you go where you've never been before."

On the way home, Mom told Aunt Matilda about Topeka, the department stores – Pelletiers, Crosby's, and the Palace – about Washburn University and its art museum, about the newly formed Topeka Civic Theatre, about the Episcopal church we attended every Sunday. She told Aunt Matilda about Lawrence, too, and Kansas City, because we had trips planned there. "We'll show you our itinerary as soon as we get home," Mom said.

"Itinerary?" asked Aunt Matilda. "I'm not a visiting diplomat, I'm on vacation."

"We'll make sure you're comfortable," said Mom. "You can do whatever you want, and skip anything you don't want to do." Mom looked at Dad. Her face meant trouble. We boys knew about the itinerary. Like the menu, it had been typed and revised and typed again.

"How about eating chocolates?" Aunt Matilda said. "Does the itinerary allow me to sit in a chair and watch these kids eat chocolates?"

"Yeah," said Richard.

"Yeah," said Robert.

"Yeah," said Randall.

Beth popped up from her seat. "I want to eat chocolates, too," she said.

Aunt Matilda laughed. "You have lovely children, Mary."

"Thank you, Aunt Matilda," said our mom.

"Matty," said Aunt Matilda for the second time that day. "I want you all to just call me Matty."

"Matty," we boys said together, "Matty, Matty, Matty." Mom and Dad refused to try it out.

When Dad pulled into our driveway we tumbled into the yard like broncos out of a chute, ready to buck the cowboy of restraint off our backs. "Change your clothes before you play!" shouted Mom.

When we came in for supper, the adults were sharing a bottle of wine and talking in the kitchen. Aunt Matilda had changed out of her rumpled blue dress and wore what our mom always called a housecoat. She sat on a kitchen chair with her thin ankles propped up on another kitchen chair. She had taken her hat off, but her hair matched her hat, a tight cap, brownish-gray, like owl feathers. She held her wineglass at her chest, inches from her lips.

"Wash your hands, it's almost time to eat," said Mom.

Dinner was Mom's special menu: a huge roast beef, cooked slow, with plenty of rare meat in the middle for the adults, enough gray outside for us children; rice cooked with onions and mushrooms and beef bouillon; green beans with bacon; and a red chocolate cake known as "Waldorf Astoria" because it originated in that glamorous New York hotel. We crowded the small table.

Aunt Matilda sat where we'd practiced, but it was different from rehearsal: we'd imagined her as a regal presence, but she sat in her striped housecoat, her chin almost at her collarbone, holding onto her wineglass for dear life, still exuding that faint stink of stale perfume, of rail smoking car, of sweat, of the moldy dust that lives in ancient, rarely packed suitcases. Mom brought steaming dishes to the table one by one, to Dad's appreciation. He stood to carve the roast beef. "Tell me when I cut the slice that looks right for you," he said to Aunt Matilda.

"Oh, whatever," she said, and the rest of us sat, mouths watering, while Dad cut slice after slice, each one bloodier than the last.

"How's this?" he asked finally.

"Anything," she said, and he dropped a piece of red meat onto the stack of plates in front of him. He loaded on the rice and the green beans and set the plate in front of her. She finished her wine and Mom stood up from the foot of the table to fill her glass. Aunt Matilda waited politely until everyone else was served, which was one of Mom's rules for us kids.

We ate like hungry boys will, our only real business being growth. Dad and Mom ate well, as they always did. Beth barely ate a scrap, but Mom had promised not to embarrass her in front of company by spending half the meal cajoling her to take one more bite of this or that. If Mom had, Beth might have pointed to Aunt Matilda and said, "But look, she's not eating anything," because she wasn't. The old woman picked at her food, pushed it around her plate, lifted only the smallest bites onto her fork, and half of that dropped to the plate before reaching her mouth. She could hardly cut her meat, the effort seeming to exhaust her; only a quick sip of wine rallied her. Through it all, Mom tried her best with small talk.

Finally, after we boys had eaten our fill, Mom turned to Aunt Matilda. "You've had a long day. Perhaps you'll enjoy your meat more in a sandwich tomorrow."

"It's a long, bumpy ride on the train," said Aunt Matilda. "I'm just glad I made it here."

Mom began clearing the plates. We boys jumped up to help. Before Mom could bring in her Waldorf Astoria cake, Aunt Matilda said, "Now I promised these children some chocolates. Richard, go to my room and you'll find a nice big box of them on my bed. You run along and bring them back."

Richard looked at Mom. She shrugged her shoulders and shot her eyes up the stairs. Richard disappeared. He returned with a narrow box of Russell Stover Assorted Chocolates.

"Now just one each," said Mom as Aunt Matilda found the cellophane string that would break the seal. She opened the box with the expertise of a magician finding still another scarf. When she lifted the lid, some of the chocolates, melted from the long, hot ride, stuck to the paper that protected them. Others sat wilted and formless, or gooed together in their little cups. "Such a trip," Aunt Matilda frowned. "Such a long and hot trip." We were afraid she might burst into tears.

Instead, she said something we were forbidden to say: "What the hell," and she burst into a laugh that embarrassed us more than tears might have. "Chocolate is chocolate, huh, boys?" she asked. "I like the nutty ones." She scooped out the wafers stuffed with peanut candy, then went for the chocolate-covered peanuts and almonds. By the time she looked up, she'd eaten six.

She launched the box around the table. "One each," Mom said again as the box reached Richard.

Richard poked at the humped centers of what was left, hoping to avoid coconut. Finally, he picked one out of the box. A thick strand of caramel pulled away from his mouth.

"Richard," said Mom.

"I can't help it," he whined.

Aunt Matilda held up her hands as though she were five years old and just finished with a brown finger painting. "See what that train did to my nice chocolates." She laughed, and when the rest of us scooped out soft chocolates and messed our hands and faces, and when Beth spit a chocolate-covered macadamia onto her plate, our parents were tolerant. Mom never served the Waldorf Astoria cake. Aunt Matilda went to her room before we kids did: "A long ride on a long train," she said.

When our mom and dad came into our room to say goodnight and tuck us in, Randall remembered the flattened coins in our suit coat pockets. "We promised her she could have them. Can we take them and say good night?"

"Absolutely not," said Dad.

"The poor woman's exhausted," said Mom. "She needs her sleep."

"How can you get tired riding on a train?" asked Robert.

"It's not just that," said our mom, "it's her age. She's almost seventy years old, you know."

"Is she going to die?" asked Randall.

"Of course not, dummy," said Richard. He had just reached the age where his brothers seemed impossibly ignorant, exactly like Beth was just growing out of the age where everything she did was cute. Robert and Randall were in between, without the obligation to be intelligent or endearing.

"I'd like to ride on the train," said Robert.

"It wouldn't make me tired," said Randall.

The next morning we woke up early. We tiptoed through the house being hushed by our mom, given stern looks by our dad, who would leave for work, then come back at noon with the rest of the day off. The breakfast menu was French toast and sausage, and we were starving. Aunt Matilda would not wake up.

We boys sent Beth to listen at the bedroom door. When she came back, we questioned her: "Can you hear her moving around? Is she snoring away?"

Beth shook her head.

"Maybe she *did* die," said Randall.

"Shut up," said Richard, "or I'm telling Mom."

At nine o'clock, Mom cracked Aunt Matilda's door. At nine thirty, Mom started cooking sausage, hoping the smell would wake Aunt Matilda and the appetite she'd lost on the train. At ten o'clock, Mom went to Aunt Matilda's door. We boys stood behind her, trying to get a peek. "Breakfast time, Aunt Matilda," said Mom.

"Matty!" insisted a voice so scratchy it sounded like a horror movie. And then, "I forgot I'm in Kansas. You get up early, don't you? Farm breakfasts, I'll bet. I'll be along."

Mom stacked French toast until it leaned precariously on the serving platter. And still no Aunt Matilda. Randall knocked on her door balancing a cup of hot coffee in his hands. "Coming," we heard, and then the door cracked open and out shuffled Aunt Matilda in a rumpled housecoat and fuzzy slippers. Her hair was plastered to the sides of her head. She leaned for the coffee. Randall backed away. Whether from the sight of her puffy eyes or her ridiculously thin legs, too insubstantial to hold her up, or the way she staggered along like she might fall on top of him, Randall turned and ran, coffee sloshing down the stairs.

Aunt Matilda didn't fall. She walked down the stairs like Beth had just quit doing, both feet meeting on each stair for balance. "Where did that boy go with my coffee?" she croaked.

"Randall," said Mom, breezing in from the kitchen with sausage and French toast. "That was Randall. He's pouring you a fresh cup."

"I've got to have black and strong. I've brought beans in my suitcase if you don't have some that'll wake me up, Mary."

"Don't worry," said Mom, "Walter likes his the same way."

Randall tiptoed to where Aunt Matilda had plunked herself at the table. "Do you drink coffee?" she asked him.

"No." He set the steaming cup next to her.

"How old are you?" she asked him.

"Eight," he said.

"You must be big for your age," she said. "I'd have guessed you to be drinking coffee and smoking cigarettes by now." She lifted the coffee to her lips with trembling hands.

"Aunt Matilda," scolded Mom as she returned to the dining room with juice and a plate of sliced apples and bananas.

"I smoked a cigarette once," said Richard.

"Richard!" Mom scolded again.

"I drank some coffee, out of Dad's cup," said Robert.

"I'm skinny for my age," Randall finally answered. "Mom and Dad worry I'm not growing enough. They think maybe there's something wrong with me."

"I wet my bed last night," said Beth.

"You children just sit down and mind your manners. And quit pestering Aunt Matilda."

"Matty," we children chanted.

The old woman smiled. "They're sweet children, Mary," she said. "Now feed them so I can watch. I love to watch young people eat."

"Do you have any kids, Aunt Matty?" asked Beth.

"Never did," said Aunt Matilda. She finished her coffee in a huge gulp, like TV cowboys drink shots in saloons. "But I have you children, and my sister's two children. Of course they're grown up now. One of them is married already."

"How is Carl?" Mom asked.

We didn't pay attention to Aunt Matilda's answer. Starving, we piled French toast on our plates, drowned it in syrup, plucked sausage straight off the serving platter into our mouths, sampled the fruit, drank glass after glass of milk. Aunt Matilda took a slice of French toast and cut it distractedly into tiny pieces while she talked about her branch of the family. Her lone piece of sausage rested on her plate like an accusatory finger, pointing at her, telling her to eat up.

After we'd cleared our places, we debated in the backyard whether she'd eaten a single bite. "I saw her," insisted Randall.

"No way," said Richard.

"Not a bit," said Robert.

"But she drank all the coffee," said Beth. "I saw Mommy empty the pot."

"I saw her take a bite," said Randall.

"I saw her sweating," said Richard.

"Who didn't," said Robert. "She kept wiping her face. We all saw that."

We ran to the car when our dad came home from work. We stormed the house together. "What's for lunch?" Dad hollered, "I'm starving." He found Mom in the kitchen, cleaning breakfast dishes.

"We just finished breakfast," said Mom. "Have what's left over."

"Where's Aunt Matilda?" He put four sausages on a slice of French toast, added another slice and took a huge bite.

"Walter," Mom frowned.

"My lunch," he said. "Even if it's not on the Matilda menu."

"It was chicken salad," said Mom. "That new recipe, with grapes."

"So where is she? After her late breakfast?"

"In her room. I encouraged her to take a bath and relax before our afternoon plans." She shook her head. The afternoon was a Topeka tour: the

Capitol, the State Historical Society Museum, Forbes Air Force Base, the Menninger Clinic, Washburn University. "Children," our mom said suddenly, as though we'd done something wrong, "go outside. Go run off your breakfasts. Right now."

We played all afternoon. We did not crowd into the Hudson, full of chicken salad. We ate peanut butter sandwiches when we pestered Mom, and were sent back outside. We did not see the Capitol, the Museum, the Base, the Clinic, the University. We did not see Aunt Matilda until dinner, when we found her sitting at the dining table, drinking wine with our parents.

She ate a little of her dinner: Swedish meatballs, the rice cooked right in with the meat, with noodles and broccoli. Just as Mom was ready to serve the Waldorf Astoria cake, Aunt Matilda, in her jolly voice, the one we hadn't heard all day, called for her chocolates. "Who went for them last night?" she asked.

"Richard," said Robert.

"Well, then it's your turn, young man," said Aunt Matilda. "The long, thin box this time, the one with the green stripes. Right on my pillow." Robert shot away like a space rocket.

They were chocolate mints, buttery, but with a bite. Aunt Matilda took several and passed the box. Richard tried to take three, but Dad cleared his throat and he put one back. The rest of us took two each, except Beth. When she reached for hers, Mom snatched the box and handed her one. "You didn't eat your broccoli," she said. Beth pouted, then ate her chocolate.

"One thing about Godiva," said Aunt Matilda, "it's sure better than broccoli." She pointed at Beth, who gave her a smile that showed teeth smeared with the rich brown of chocolate. Dad poured the last of the wine into her glass. She raised it and said, "Here's to your wonderful family."

Aunt Matilda slept in the next day, and the next. The itinerary, freshly typed on clean white paper, sat on the living room desk. Dad stayed later and later at work, since it was no use coming home to find Aunt Matilda "relaxing" in her room. We kids didn't care. We had Waldorf Astoria cake for lunch and afternoon snack. We roamed the neighborhood instead of being squeezed into the car and driven to boring places we'd already visited too many times.

But by the end of the week, we realized we were going to miss the Kansas City Zoo. "You promised us we could go," we told Mom on the last day of Aunt Matilda's visit.

"I can't force your great-aunt to do anything," she said.

"Will she ever wake up?" we asked.

"Maybe by ten o'clock," said Mom.

"Can we wake her up?" asked Randall.

"At ten you can go to her door and knock gently."

But ten o'clock came, and we knocked as loud as we dared. We stood in the hall listening to the nothing behind Aunt Matilda's door.

"Let's pretend to be animals," said Robert. "I'm an elephant." He bent over, threw his arm over his head for a trunk, and paced the floor outside Aunt Matilda's door. Every few steps he reared back and his elephant trumpeted furiously.

"I'm a lion," said Richard. He dropped to all fours and crawled on the floor, head held high. He roared from deep in his chest.

"I'm a crocodile," said Randall. He dropped to his belly and snapped his teeth. He hissed at the elephant and the lion.

"I want to be a kitty," said Beth. She pranced and meowed.

Robert stood up out of his crouch. "There aren't kittens at the zoo," he said. "I wanted us to be zoo animals." He trumpeted, and raised his voice. "I want to go to the zoo!"

We meowed and hissed and roared until Mom shooed us outside. By the time she called us in for lunch, we knew we weren't going to Kansas City. Aunt Matilda sat at the table drinking cup after cup of coffee, exactly like nothing was wrong.

"When I grow up," said Richard, "I'm going to go wherever I want to go."

"I'm going to do what I want," said Robert.

"I'm going to be a zookeeper," said Randall, "and be a lion tamer, too."

"Are we going to the zoo?" asked Beth.

"Oh, dear," said Aunt Matilda, "was it the zoo today?" She tried to smile, but it was more like a pinch in her owlish face.

Richard hurried away from the table and returned with the itinerary. We weren't sure Aunt Matilda had ever seen it. He put it next to her. "Let me see," she said. But as she reached for it, she elbowed her coffee, and the cup tumbled over. The coffee streamed over the itinerary. Aunt Matilda broke into a sweat. The room smelled sour, like bad cottage cheese. Aunt Matilda tried to pat at the stain with her napkin. Mom brought in a sponge. "I'm sorry," said Aunt Matilda, "I'm sure the zoo would have been just lovely."

"It's in Swope Park," said Richard.

"It's great big," said Randall.

"It's got a train," said Robert.

"Have I ever been?" asked Beth.

"We can go anytime," said Mom.

In fact, we'd only been once. But because of the way she bit her lip, because of the wrinkles in her high forehead, because of the disappointment in her face, we didn't challenge Mom. She was just like us: we'd all waited for Aunt Matilda to wake up, waited to see if she would eat, waited to see what she'd be "up to" for the afternoon. Then dinner and chocolates and she would disappear for the evening.

That night, at dinner, Dad was jolly. It was Aunt Matilda's last night with us. Maybe he was glad. He taught us to toast, with grape juice in small tumblers. We clinked them against the adults' wineglasses as Dad said nice words about Aunt Matilda and our mom's side of the family. Aunt Matilda responded with "fine children" and "beautiful home" and "fine community. I like Kansas, too," she said.

We shook our heads. Maybe it didn't matter in a toast if you told the truth, we thought, and Richard cleared his throat in an imitation of Dad: "To all the fun we had this week." We clinked.

Robert cleared his throat. "To Aunt Matilda's chocolates."

Randall raised his tumbler. "To Mom's big breakfasts."

Then Beth lifted her glass, but she didn't have any grape juice left. She looked around at everyone, but she didn't know what to say. She thumped her glass down, ready to burst into tears.

"Thank God you didn't say anything," said Aunt Matilda. She leaned forward and poured a tiny bit of wine into Beth's glass. "It's bad luck to toast with an empty glass."

"The child shouldn't have wine," said Mom, but it was too late. Beth took a sip. She made a sour face, but she swallowed.

"I want some," said Richard.

"Me, too," said Robert.

"I get some, too," said Randall.

We gulped our grape juice and held out our glasses. Aunt Matilda sloshed a tiny bit of wine into each eager glass. We sipped it down before our parents stopped us. It was sour and pungent, like the smell that followed Aunt Matilda around the house, but it made our mouths warm. Our tummies burned.

"More," said Richard, but nobody took him seriously.

"There is no more," said Dad.

"And I'm out of chocolates," said Aunt Matilda. "It must be getting time for me to go home."

"Tomorrow," said Beth.

Aunt Matilda went to bed right after dinner. "Long train ride," she said.

We boys went to our room at nine o'clock. We lay in the dark, trying for sleep, but we were keyed up, as though we were the ones traveling on the train the next day. "Your bed is going to be full of cooties," Randall said to Richard.

"Shut up," said Richard.

"I wouldn't want to sleep in your room after she's been in there. It stinks," Robert said.

"Yeah, it stinks," said Randall. It was the revenge of the little brothers, the two who had to share a room jealous of the one who had his own room. "She's probably in there snoring away and filling the bed with her cooties."

"She gave us chocolates every night," said Richard.

"She sat around in those old floppy clothes and let out a stink," said Robert.

"She ran out of chocolates," said Randall.

"I bet she didn't," said Robert. "I bet there's a bunch of them. She's just saving them for the train."

"I wish I had one," said Randall. "Right now."

"Me, too," said Robert. "I'm not sleepy anyway."

"I dare you to go look," said Randall. He slapped his hand against the side of Richard's bed.

"Why should I go?" asked Richard. "It's not my idea."

"It's your room," said Robert. "You can go in looking for something. A book, or your slippers or something."

"I won't go unless you guys come with me," said Richard.

"Mom and Dad will catch us," Robert said.

"Yeah," said Randall, "the more of us, the more we get caught."

"You're chicken," said Richard. "You're just scared to go in there when Aunt Matilda's asleep."

"Am not," said Randall.

"Are too," said Robert. "You're afraid she'll wake up and catch you and eat you up. You're afraid she's a witch."

"You're afraid she's a zombie," said Richard. It was the revenge of the older brothers, the two who were supposed to be brave taunting the youngest for his cowardice in order to build up their own courage.

"I dare both of you," said Robert, the middle brother trying to play both ends off each other.

"We all go, or nobody goes," said Richard. "I don't even care about chocolates."

"Chicken," said Randall.

"Double chicken," said Robert.

"Triple chicken," said Richard. He stood up out of bed. We tiptoed down the brightly lit hall, past our parents' bedroom. We stood outside Aunt Matilda's door. We bent down, placed our ears to the thin wood. We heard the rhythm of caught breath followed by the short rasp of a snore. Richard reached for the door handle, and we quietly spilled into the room. A crack of light from the hall creased through the room, revealed the shadow of Aunt Matilda's suitcase next to the bed, closed up like some huge sleeping turtle, revealed part of the bed, part of her. When we looked, to see if she was still sound asleep, we were amazed. Lying in her bed, still in one of her old housecoats, she seemed unnaturally short, shrunken up. Her feet were so tiny they might have been a child's. Her most prominent feature was her mouth, wide open, catching, then rasping breath.

As we approached the suitcase, each of us broke the light, made a momentary shadow cross Aunt Matilda's face. She moved slightly, her body shaking like a dog's when it dreams. We stopped, terrified. Her smell engulfed us, a sour smell, like the insides of our mouths after drinking wine, before we brushed our teeth. We hurried to the suitcase. Richard bent over it and reached for the snaps. Robert put his finger to his lips. Randall crouched behind, holding his ears, as though that would help silence. When

Richard released the clasps, they snapped up with the sound of a turtle biting the air. We waited, forcing ourselves to breathe. Richard opened the suitcase. Right on the top was a thin box of chocolates. Robert started to turn back, pushing Randall, but Richard grabbed his arm. Richard dug into the suitcase and pulled up two more boxes of chocolates, one with stripes on it like the mint box Aunt Matilda had shared with us earlier in the week. The other was thick, the kind that opened like a book.

We could have left then, but Richard dug some more. This time, he found something hard and gleaming when he held it, something that clinked against the first when he picked up the second, something that shattered the silence of the bedroom when he dropped a third onto the second in the pile of Aunt Matilda's frumpy housecoats and underpants. The striking of glass against glass made a thundering toast. We knew the liquid inside the bottles was something people toasted with, that Aunt Matilda had probably toasted herself in her room night after night, or in the early morning when she wouldn't come out. Richard tried to bury the bottles, but they made too much noise, as bad as marbles in a bathtub.

Aunt Matilda turned to the wall, then onto her back again. We trembled, but she didn't open her eyes. When she settled back into a snore, we saw that one flap of her housecoat, which was unbuttoned halfway, had fallen away from her body. One of her thin legs was exposed, bare all the way up and past her waist.

Randall stopped breathing. Robert turned away. Richard stood and stared, because none of us boys had seen before what we saw then: the mound of pubic hair, thin and disheveled, the naked thigh, the dark space between Aunt Matilda's legs.

Who knows how long we would have stayed in the bedroom, staring and not staring, frightened and curious. But we thought we heard a noise in our parents' room next door. We ducked down. Richard dropped the boxes of chocolate into the suitcase, but he didn't bother to snap it shut. We ran out of Aunt Matilda's room.

"Boys," Dad said. His head peeked out from his door.

"We had to go to the bathroom," said Richard.

"All three of you? At the same time?"

"Yes, sir," said Robert.

"Really bad," said Randall.

Dad smiled. "Well, go to bed. I don't want to hear another peep out of you boys tonight."

We did as we were told.

On the way to the train the next morning, the one morning Aunt Matilda actually ate some breakfast, the car was as quiet as our bedroom the night before, when each of us lay wrapped in sheets, and in thoughts we didn't share. And we stood quietly on the platform waiting for Aunt Matilda's train to charge the station. None of us could look at Aunt Matilda, so we stared down the tracks to where distance forced the parallel rails together.

When the train finally rumbled toward us, Aunt Matilda, dressed in her very best, looking again like a traveler and not a wrinkled bird in a house-coat, turned to us. She set down her handbag and pulled out a box of mints. "I was wrong," she said. "I rummaged around in my suitcase and found more chocolates. For you, boys." She offered the box to Richard. When he reached for it, she clamped down on his hand. "Just one thing, young men," she said. She looked at our mother and father and we gulped. Richard stood beside her, his hand on the box of mints. Robert and Randall wanted to run, anywhere, up the tracks or down. But finally, as she wanted us to, the three of us looked Aunt Matilda in the eye. "You boys never gave me those coins you promised me," she said.

"Coins!" shouted Richard.

"Yeah, coins," repeated Robert.

Randall reached hopefully into his suit coat pocket, then grinned. He pulled out the flat piece of copper, and we knew we would find our coins, too. We hadn't been anywhere that whole week, not church, not to Kansas City, nowhere we could wear our best clothes. We offered what had been a dime, a nickel, and a penny to Aunt Matilda, and she let go of the chocolate mints. We ran in circles as fast as we could, relieved by what she had de-manded of us, relieved by what she hadn't said to us, and to our parents.

"You and Walter have a lovely home." Aunt Matilda nodded definitely, so that her feathered hat almost wobbled off her head. "And a lovely family, too."

"Thank you so much for visiting, Aunt Matilda," said Mom, but she sounded like the minister after church.

"Please come again, Aunt Matilda," said our dad, "anytime."

"Matty," said Aunt Matilda. "How was I to know you'd be so formal out here in the West?" The train hissed, the conductors set out their stools, people disembarked around us. Aunt Matilda took one last look at Mom, then backed toward the passenger car. "You've been good to put up with me," she said.

Our parents stood silent, waiting.

Aunt Matilda turned to mount the stool. Beth pumped her short legs into action. "Matty!" she shrieked, her voice so loud we imagined Matty was one of her dolls with its head under the train wheel. Beth almost tackled Aunt Matilda with an extravagant hug. Mom peeled her away, and Aunt Matilda slowly climbed into the train. Her slip showed three inches of white below her knees. When she turned for a final wave, she looked one last time at us boys. She crooked her finger and shook it at us. "You boys eat those mints one at a time," she said in perfect imitation of our mother.

"No!" said Richard.

"All at once!" shouted Robert.

"Thank you, Matty," yelled Randall. He waved furiously.

The old woman disappeared into the train. We hurried to the Hudson. On the way home, Richard tore open the box of mints. Mom didn't say a word. Each of us took as many as we could lift out. Richard passed them up to the front seat, but only Beth took any. We boys finished the box before Dad pulled into our drive.

We were glad to be home, to be stuffed with chocolates, to know what we knew. We were smug, in our innocence, to think we were the only ones who knew it. We ran into the house, screaming.

"Matty?" yelled Richard

"Matty?" shouted Robert.

"Matty?" screamed Randall.

But, of course, nobody answered back. Nobody said a word.

Topeka Underground

The whole time I was growing up, the Lindsborgs' unfinished house sat in our newly created suburban development. The basement-foundation cinder blocks rose up three high. Window wells cupped dirty windows never open to the light. Nothing but the faintest glow came from them, even at night. The top of the foundation was black with tarpaper. When Mr. Lindsborg papered his roof-floor, winter soon followed. For a year after my family moved onto the block, I didn't even see the Lindsborgs. They did not own an automobile. They did not work in their yard, but let it grow to knee-high weeds good for hide and seek.

We kids did not trick-or-treat there on Halloween because we weren't sure how to knock on their huge cellar door, painted white, hinged on both sides to open in the middle, like storm cellar doors, or like the entrance to a homesteader's storage cave. In winter, we saw a plume of smoke rise from a short tin spout, topped with the tin man's hat, and sticking up from the foundation. We saw the Lindsborgs' footprints, one set very large, the other very small, both in boots, come from the house to the woodpile and back again; once, down the street to meet tire tracks and then back home.

One day, in the spring of my fifth-grade year, I cut the center of the neighborhood lengthwise, on my slow way to school. That meant moving between the Lindsborgs' woodpile and the one fence on the block, the chain link of their back neighbor, who wanted to express a solid difference between his green, clipped yard and the riot of dandelion, pigweed, lamb's-quarter, bindweed, and wild grasses growing unchecked on the Lindsborgs' property. Just when I was at the end of the long, stacked pile of wood, the cellar door screeched open. I ducked behind the woodpile.

Mr. Lindsborg climbed, stooped, up the outside basement stairs, shaking his head slowly like an old bear remembering the world after a long winter. His beard was white, and longer and fuller than any department store Santa

Claus's, but streaked with yellow. I saw why when he reared his head to spit tobacco juice at his heavy boots.

Then he came toward me, moving slowly, as though reminding his limbs how to work. I could outrun him if I had to, so I stayed to watch. At the opposite side and end of the woodpile, he stood quietly. I heard a stream against grass, a sound I could not believe, but had to acknowledge. Mr. Lindsborg was peeing in his yard, something I hadn't done since I was five years old. I stayed tucked down, hidden, wanting to run, but not daring to, now, until it was quiet again.

Mr. Lindsborg chucked wood into a stack on his arm and started toward his basement. I peeked out at his back, hunched now with the weight of a morning's warmth. Just as he reached his cellar doors, thrown back like the stiff covers of an open book, he muttered, his voice garbled and incoherent. A very small head appeared from the basement stairwell. Mrs. Lindsborg wore a blue kerchief tied in a knot under her chin, and when she reached to help with the wood, I saw such thin arms, like small sticks, like the arms of a child. Just before grasping a small piece of stove wood, that arm waved at me, and the small mouth smiled, and I ran like hell for school.

Once I'd seen the Lindsborgs, and Mrs. Lindsborg had seen me, I wanted to see them again. I asked my parents about them. "Don't bother them, William," said my mother. "They're old. And I've heard she has some disease."

She's so small, I almost blurted out, smaller than me.

"I heard he bought his lot off old Mr. Daniels," said my father. "They're friends or something. It was before Daniels sold the rest of his farm to Stevens. Before there was even a Nottingham Street here."

I excused myself from the table. I knew my father's speech about property values and old Mr. Daniels's paint-chipped house, his rundown barn, his crumpling boxcar full of ancient bales of hay: How his four-lot "farm," littered with old cutters and rakes, plows and disks, and meager, head-high corn ought to be sold, torn down and developed, like the rest of the neighborhood.

I told my friend Manny Stein about seeing the Lindsborgs. We were in our hideout in the bottom of his bomb shelter, where we went to pretend the world was ended and we were the only ones left.

"That old man's not one of the ones we're letting in," Manny said. He raised his extended finger as though pointing a gun. "Pow, pow," he said, using the pistol in his head that matched the one in his father's closet. He took a few small bullets out of their box in the bomb shelter. "This one's for him, and here's one for his old lady."

We both knew that when the bomb dropped, everybody would head for Manny's shelter. We would kill them all to keep the food, water, and air for ourselves. We liked to sit in the bright light of the hundred-watt bulb, the smooth concrete walls cool as the inside of an empty test tube around us, and imagine the end, more like a wonderful beginning: two boys, alone, ready to start the world over again.

But when I wasn't with Manny or some other friend, I drifted again and again to the Lindsborg foundation. Even though I tried, I didn't see the Lindsborgs until early one Sunday, just after dawn. Out retrieving the paper for my father, I heard the cellar doors creak open three houses up. I slapped the paper onto the porch and took out on my bicycle. I left it in the Lindsborgs' unpaved driveway and sneaked to the short wall their foundation made. They were in back. Each had a bag. Each stooped to the ground to fill the bag with something. With dandelion tops.

"Come," said Mrs. Lindsborg suddenly, and she turned to wave to me. "You will help?" she asked. She was no bigger than I was, with a smile on her face; she might have been a new girl on the playground.

I shrugged my shoulders and started toward them. Mr. Lindsborg looked at me sternly, his lips pursed under his large white mustache. His back was hunched under his bib overalls. But I approached him, with both curiosity and fear. Finally, he held out his bag and muttered something from the back of his throat.

Mrs. Lindsborg circled around him, her legs stiff, so she looked as though she was walking on stilts. "Dandelions," she said. "We pick the tops, with no green, while the dew sits on them."

I did not know what to say. Picking dandelions was for children. We waited until the yellow turned to white, and the seeds mushroomed onto the plant top, poised and ready to catch the wind of our breaths. But I reached down and picked a yellow top. I took it to Mrs. Lindsborg's bag. "My name is William," I said.

"William," she said, nodding her head. She reached for the single top in my hand. "Too much green," she said. "Nothing but yellow, or the wine will turn bitter."

"Wine?" I asked.

"Dandelion wine," she said. Mr. Lindsborg grunted, smiling. Then he licked his lips and patted his large stomach.

"How do you make it?" I asked him.

"He cannot hear you," Mrs. Lindsborg said. "I am his ears, and his voice. When he talks, only I can understand the sounds he makes."

I looked at Mr. Lindsborg, who hadn't heard what she said. He smiled, as though still thinking of the wine they would make. I picked another dandelion top. This time, it passed inspection, and Mrs. Lindsborg dropped it into her cloth bag.

"Sweet," she said. "When winter is cold the wine will be our spring." She hobbled from place to place, barely able to bend her stiff body, almost creaking on the hinge of her sunken waist. The more I watched her, the faster I picked, careening around her like a crazed insect.

Until I heard my name, faintly called into the early Sunday morning air. "I gotta go," I said.

"Thank you, William," said Mrs. Lindsborg. "You shall have a taste of wine, come winter."

I ran for my bike. Mr. Lindsborg grunted after me, and I turned to wave to him before I pedaled to my split-level house down the street.

"I've been riding my bike," I told my father.

"Are you forgetting we go to church?" asked my mother.

"No," I said, but I had forgotten everything but racing from one yellow dandelion top to another, filling Mrs. Lindsborg's sack.

From that morning when I officially met the Lindsborgs, I spent the rest of my spring looking for them. Sometimes I would carry a stack of logs from the woodpile to their cellar door. The next day I would find a large sheet of paper between two logs, with "Thank you, William" scrawled on it. Sometimes I would catch them in their yard in the very early morning, before the birds were even awake. Once, they were harvesting lamb's-quarter for a salad. When their large redbud bloomed, Mrs. Lindsborg showed me how to pick and eat the tiny pink flowers. She gathered enough for what looked like a whole meal.

Each time I saw them, out early, or on my way to school, or at dusk, just before I heard my name called into the clear evening air, they greeted me as though we'd known each other for years, Mrs. Lindsborg with "Hello, William," and Mr. Lindsborg with a generous shake of his head and a smile of brown, tobacco-stained teeth. They always wore the same clothing: he in overalls and a stiff flannel shirt; she in a blue kerchief, long blue dress of some thick material, covered over by a deep blue shawl. She always carefully explained what they were doing; I helped for a time, then they went inside.

I wanted to follow them but was too timid to ask. Still, I prepared for the time when they would invite me into their basement. I'd practiced saying, "Yes, but just for a minute," because I was frightened. Manny Stein said the Lindsborgs tempted children into their basement, suffocated them, drained out all their blood, and stacked them in a closet like Egyptian mummies. They did this because they had no children of their own. Other kids said their whole basement smelled horrible, because they had no bathroom. They just went on the floor in a corner like cats and dogs, and they'd move out once their basement was full and there was no room to live in. And, of course, my parents had always told me, "Never go in the house of someone you don't know." Mom and Dad would expect me to come home and ask their permission, but I knew I wouldn't.

On the first day of summer, with long playing days ahead of me, I went to the Lindsborgs' yard. Their cellar door was closed. No smoke plumed from their chimney. Since they didn't own a car, I could never tell if they were home. The grass was as tall as my knees, and grasshoppers clung to the leaves and stems, sometimes hopping onto my bare legs. In my hands, when I caught them, they spit their filthy brown juice, trying to soften, then eat, my palm. I cupped them, then let them fly away, their ratchety wings too insubstantial to keep them from falling.

I felt I had to see the Lindsborgs to start my summer right. Next year I would be in sixth grade, one of the big kids. Our teacher told us to prepare ourselves over the summer. We would be the models everyone else looked up to. My parents had sat me down the week before and decided on Boy

Scout camp for a week, swimming lessons until I passed the advanced class, and some art lessons especially for kids, offered by the local college. "It's going to be a great summer," said my dad. "Expensive, but fun."

"It'll be a summer of fun learning," said my mom.

I had never knocked on the Lindsborgs' door. As far as I knew, nobody ever had, or would. So I did. I went to the cellar door and bent down on my bare knees in the grass and rapped on the wood. I stood up and waited.

After a time I bent down again, but this time I pounded with my fist.

Then I whapped on the door with my tennis shoe. It seemed to give, as though it might not be latched solidly from the inside. I reached for the metal handle and pulled. Up came the door, screeching on its hinges. I looked down the concrete stairwell at another door, white-painted wood, latched from the outside with a small hook and eye. They were not home. I went down the stairs to see if I could peek inside through the glass panes. I had no intention of lifting the hook out of the eye and turning the doorknob until I did it.

Their basement was one big room, lit only by the dull light from the window wells. I stood squeezing the summer sun from my eyes, like when my parents took me to a matinee. When I finally opened my eyes, I was in another world. Around me, the walls were hung with quilts of intricate pattern: circles, swirls, blocks, triangles, diamonds, fans, all pieced in an unceasing movement of wheeling colors. The furniture was huge and dark: a hutch stacked with delicate, almost paper-thin china; two elegantly carved wardrobes, buttressing the walls in a corner; a canopy bed, like in the princess's bedroom of a castle, curtained so that the inside was a little room, closed today, like the basement had been.

In another corner was the kitchen: freestanding sink; huge iron cookstove, shiny with blacking; small oak table with two chairs; shelf after shelf of food in jars – the glowing red of tomatoes, the dull green of cooked beans and dill pickles, the deep purple of beets, the yellow of summer squash and corn, the white of pearl onions, the orange of pumpkin, the colors as patterned and lovely as the quilts.

Still another corner was a workshop: several tables were littered with blocks of wood, hand tools, and wood shavings; raw lumber leaned against the wall. When I turned to look more closely, shelf after shelf of wood carvings – men, women, children, and more animals than in a circus – stared back at me. Even in the dull light of the open door, I saw intricate detail: the teeth of smiling children, the bold stripes of a zebra, the wrinkles of an elephant's trunk, the teats of a sow. Each carving was perfect and alive, but everything was exactly the same size, as though cut from the same block of wood: a woman holding a child in her lap was no smaller than the hippopotamus next to her, who was no bigger than the grasshopper, who was no smaller than the deer at the back of that parade across Mr. Lindsborg's shelf.

On the far wall, near the bed, was the only door: to the bathroom, I supposed. I went to see. The old porcelain fixtures stood like ghosts in the near dark. The side opposite the bathroom fixtures was given to storage: linens, jars, more wood, old furniture, boxes, all neatly arranged. The inside of the Lindsborgs' basement was as tidy as the outside of their place was given to disorder.

The whole time I was in their house I felt no fear, just curiosity, like Goldilocks exploring the home of the three bears. Once inside, in fact, I was disappointed. There were no horrible secrets to discover, no children's bodies, no terrible smells, nothing but intricate simplicity, honesty of work, and obvious care for every detail. The difference between the Lindsborgs' basement and other houses I'd been in was remarkable; they were people like nobody else I knew or would know. But the experience of peeking into their foundation had all the silly adventure of spending the night in a tent in my own backyard. I hurried away, hooking the eye in the door after me, screeching the cellar doors closed, then running until I was out of their yard.

That's when I heard the sirens. Frightened, I hurried to Manny Stein's house and hid behind the closed hatch of the bomb shelter to watch. An ambulance pulled into the Lindsborgs' graveled driveway. Two attendants raced for a stretcher, jerked it to their shoulders, and hurried to the cellar door. Mr. Lindsborg appeared from up the street, no doubt from Mr. Daniels's farm. He signaled the men to go down the stairs, and they disappeared.

They didn't come up for a long time. I kneeled there behind the funny mushroom cap of our hideout. I heard my name called over and over again, my mother's voice insistent, but not as compelling as my need to wait.

Later, she told me she was afraid the ambulance was for one of us neighborhood kids, hit by a car or injured terribly climbing trees. I just shook my head.

I didn't tell her how, after what seemed forever, the men appeared up the stairwell, the stretcher between them, the small body on it, covered completely by a white sheet, the old man trudging behind, muttering, his garbled voice barely reaching my ears.

I didn't tell her how, when they got to the ambulance, Mr. Lindsborg was told he couldn't go with them, how he howled and pounded the vehicle with his huge hands.

I didn't tell her how, when the ambulance drove away, Mr. Lindsborg sat on his foundation and cried, or how I cried, too.

I didn't tell her how, on the way to the bathroom in the Lindsborgs' foundation home, I had been so tempted to open the curtains that surrounded their huge, four-poster canopy bed, to look where they slept, though I have done it many times, in my dreams, since.

"Maybe he'll give up and sell his ugly foundation," my father said at dinner.

"I hope he doesn't," I said. "I hope he always lives there."

"You're still a kid," said my father. "You'll see it different when you get older."

I never did see it different. I never told my father how, that next winter, on my way home from school, I saw Mr. Lindsborg at his woodpile, how he waved to me and yodeled in the way he did when trying to speak. How when I waved back and went to him, he clasped me to him, hugging me. When I broke free I saw tears in his old gray eyes. He reached into his overalls pocket and gave me a small vial, an old medicine bottle, stopped with a tiny cork and containing a pale yellow liquid. Mr. Lindsborg made a noise I understood as "drink." He kept saying it, then throwing back his head and putting his thumb to his mouth.

I uncorked that tiny bottle and drank the sweet liquid, the taste like earthy lemonade, only lighter, with the twist of alcohol to make me catch my breath. It was dandelion wine. I remembered the spring, and Mrs. Lindsborg. I handed him the vial, and mouthed a big "Thank you." I moved my head up and down, and he nodded back, trying to smile.

Just as I tried to run away, Mr. Lindsborg grabbed my arm and reached into his overalls again. This time he pulled out a carving, smaller than the ones I'd seen on his shelf when I'd trespassed in his basement. In a circle of wood the size of my hand, two snakes, mouths to tails, consumed each other. Their eyes bulged, each anticipating the slow swallowing of the other. "Thank you," I said, nodding again, and ran for home.

I stopped in my yard, in the little gardening shed my father had built out back, and hid the snakes behind a shovel. Later, I buried them in the yard, just to the side of one of my father's rosebushes. I didn't want to mix my knowledge of Mr. Lindsborg with my parents' curiosity. They were just counting the years until he moved away.

Farmer Daniels moved first. Manny Stein and I were in the old crumpled boxcar one day, trying out cigarettes for the first time the summer before junior high. Maybe one of us left a smoldering butt by mistake. Maybe Manny, who left after I did, deliberately set the fire. He never told me. Sirens roared up our street, and the neighborhood came to watch what turned out to be a huge, but harmless, bonfire. I was more alarmed than the adults, who seemed somehow relieved.

Mr. Daniels moved into a nursing home the next week. His children said he was too forgetful to take care of himself. They sold the rest of his tiny farm to the developer, and four Tudor homes, oversized for their lots, moved into the neighborhood.

I never saw Mr. Lindsborg again. Manny and I quit playing the kinds of games that took us through backyard lots. We needed playing fields. His father sheered the top off the bomb shelter and filled it with cement. The whole neighborhood grew up: people put in privacy fences, hedgerows, chain link fence, shrubbery. Mr. Lindsborg's foundation sat unchanged, except for a new layer of tarpaper each fall.

Then one summer, when I returned from college, his house was finished. "There were three huge boys," said my mother. "The spitting image of Lindsborg, all in overalls, with beards. They came with trucks full of lumber and put up his house in three weeks. Then they were inside doing the finish work. Never said a word to any of us."

"Typical," said my father. "But they did a heck of a nice job for amateurs."

The next spring, the newly built frame house was sold. Nobody said goodbye to Mr. Lindsborg. People wondered for a while just what kind of people would move into the house, but the new neighbors seemed like ordinary folks, oblivious to the history of the Lindsborg place. Pretty soon everybody took them a cake or casserole, and a story or two about the Lindsborgs.

I stayed away. I did dig up the carving. It looked so much like an old root I was surprised it hadn't sprouted. The detail was all gone, but I knew what it was, and I took it with me to remind me of life underground.

During the Twelfth Summer of Elmer D. Peterson

Elmer hated his name. He always had. But now he hated it even more. He hated the farm his parents had moved him to. He hated the country. He hated not being able to ride his bike. He hated not having any friends.

Actually, since June 1st, he'd hated even being Elmer D. Peterson. June 1st was the day his father quit his electrician's job for good. That was the day they'd moved out into the middle of nowhere, Wabaunsee County, Kansas, for good. That was the day he'd done his last run with the Sunflower Track Club and quit the team for good. That was the day everything went bad. For good!

Now there was nothing to do but help his parents. Out here, they didn't have cable TV. They didn't have people his age to run track with. They didn't even have a track near enough to run on regularly. They didn't have a good paved road near enough to ride his touring bicycle on. They didn't have anything but sky and grass and work.

"Rise and shine!" his father yelled up the attic stairs every morning.

"No way!" he shouted back.

His dad gave him time. So did his Mom. It was the least they could do for a kid they'd named Elmer, and then ruined for life, moving him away from everything he'd ever known, including all the friends he'd just finished fifth grade with.

Time was moving slow. His dad was like a little kid, excited and happy. "There aren't enough hours in the day," his father said every night at the supper table. Elmer thought there were way too many hours in the day.

He complained that there was nothing to do. "Explore," his mother said to him every morning. Elmer thought there was nothing to explore. He'd seen the fields, and the creek, and the woods, and all the outbuildings. There wasn't anything else. There never would be anything else. His life was completely and totally ruined.

Then, on July 4th, early in the morning, something happened. From his attic window, Elmer D. Peterson watched an old man with a crooked back lead a small, very thick horse down the gravel road toward his house. The two of them looked like a yo-yo. The old man would hobble out ten feet, turn around, then stand there jerking on the rope until the horse ran up to him, almost attacking him, circling him, and then standing very still, only his tail twitching.

Elmer ignored his mother's call to breakfast. He wanted to see what would happen. He hoped the man was bringing the horse to them. He didn't know why the old man would, but still he hoped. And then, sure enough, horse and man turned into their lane. Elmer ran downstairs.

"Whoa," said his father. "What's got into you?"

But Elmer was halfway down the lane before his father caught up with him. The old man stood squinting at them, his eyes the same burnt umber as the tobacco juice running down his stubbly chin.

"Well," said the old man, "do me a favor. I can't keep this no-good horse. He's busted the fence. You keep him until I can get it fixed."

Elmer approached the horse. Cockleburs tangled its black mane. Elmer reached out to touch the horse's twitching withers.

The old man suddenly jerked the little horse's head down. "Don't you even think about it, you piece of glue," he snarled. Elmer backed away. The old man looked at Elmer's dad. "Just over the holiday," he said. "Your boy here can feed him." The old man spat and looked at Elmer. "Would you like that, boy?"

"Sure," said Elmer. "Can we, Dad? Please?"

"No food," said Elmer's dad. "No equipment. No decent fence here."

"You got that corral there, I ain't blind," said the old man. He pulled the little horse close to him. "A good critter, really. Part Shetland pony, part Morgan horse. Was broke just as gentle as a rocking chair, once. Had all my little grandbabies up on his back. No bit, just halter broke. We all get hard times, you know."

"All right," said Elmer's dad.

The old man went straight back through the old gate to the corral. He tied the thick little Morgan to a post, promised to return, and limped away down the road. Elmer's dad went inside. Elmer's mom called him for breakfast. He stayed with the horse as long as he could, but he didn't want his mom mad at him.

"I'll feed him and water him, and I'll even find an old comb and get the tangles out of his mane. I'll call him Tangler," Elmer said.

"Don't name him, son," said Elmer's dad. "He's not yours."

"Just for while he's here. Just for a while. I'm calling him Tangler," Elmer insisted.

His father frowned. His mother sighed. But neither said a word.

Then they heard a terrific clatter from the corral. Elmer was the first to the kitchen door. Tangler was rearing back, arching away from the post, shaking his head and whinnying, his front hooves pawing the air. Then the rope snapped, and Tangler, tail extended, galloped in one quick circle around the corral and went straight for the gate. It was as tall as he was, but he sailed over it as though he'd sprouted wings. Elmer's father ran to the lane, but Tangler reached the road in a flurry of dust, turned in the direction he'd come, and literally high-tailed it out of there.

Elmer's dad picked up a rock and heaved it as far as he could. "Good riddance," he shouted.

"Don't," said Elmer's mother, and went inside.

Elmer just stood in the doorway. He was sorry Tangler was gone. He was sorry his father didn't care. But he wasn't sorry he'd seen Tangler soar like an eagle over the fence, seen those powerful legs churn down the lane, seen that smooth gallop of freedom. Tangler was faster than Elmer imagined any creature could be.

After breakfast, he went to his room and found his old racing flats in the back of his closet. He put them on and hurried down the stairs.

"Whoa," said his father. "Where are you going?"

"Scouting," he said. Then, looking at his mother, he said, "Exploring." He was out the door before either could call him back. He was running, faster than he remembered he could, down the lane, onto the road, and away. After Tangler.

Elmer didn't return until lunch. In all that time he saw Tangler only once. He came to the top of a rise, a place where he could see two miles in every direction. He stopped running. He put his hands on his thin hips and bent forward slightly, breathing deeply, catching his breath. If he hadn't been leaning forward, he wouldn't have seen the horse, surprisingly close to him, almost hidden in a clump of brush in a pasture.

Tangler saw him. The horse whinnied, and trotted deeper into the brush that follows every draw into a creek or pond. Elmer scooted under the fence, scraping his bare knees on a jagged shelf of rock. He ran carefully cross-country, into the brush and down the draw, but he didn't see Tangler. He managed to fill his T-shirt with stick-tights and other small seeds that take passage all through the long summer, hoping to find new homes in fresh soil.

At home, he filled a quart jar with water and drank it all before he said a word. "I know where Tangler is," he said finally.

"I don't care where he is," said Elmer's dad. "He's not our horse."

"We said we'd keep him," Elmer insisted. "We promised to feed him. You said I could take care of him."

"I'm not going to buy feed for a horse I've only seen for five minutes, Elmer. It just doesn't make sense."

"We can catch him."

"No," said Elmer's dad. He crossed his arms on his chest, something he did when he meant business.

Elmer sat down, frowning.

"We're going to the Andersons' at three," Elmer's dad reminded him.

"Not me," said Elmer. "I'm finding Tangler."

"You'll be ready at three o'clock, young man, or you'll never see that horse again."

"Yes, sir," said Elmer.

After lunch he went up to his room and looked out his attic window, first to the north, then to the south. As far as he could see all around him, miles of green hills, with their rock outcroppings, the lines of trees revealing fence lines and other farms, the brown ribbons of road trailing off in the four directions, he could not see Tangler.

His mother sat on his bed.

"I wish I had a horse," Elmer said.

"Your father and I wish you did, too," she said.

"Then why can't I?"

"Elmer," she sighed. "We don't have the fences fixed. We don't have the time it would take to really care for a horse. We don't have a cent of extra money. You know we're taking a gamble even being out here. But it's very important to your father."

"He doesn't care about me. He only pays attention to what's important."

"You're important, Elmer. He's just worried. About money. About getting enough done before winter. He's just like you. He's doing things he's never done before. You know that's not easy."

"Can I go look for Tangler some more?"

"If you're back by three o'clock sharp."

Elmer was tired of running. He put on long pants and walked slowly through fields in the direction he'd seen Tangler. Along the way he picked up stones to see how far he could hurl them. He followed their arc first with his eyes, then with his feet, hoping to find the exact same stones again. He never did. He had about as much chance of that as he did of seeing Tangler again.

Once, one of his rocks disturbed a red-tailed hawk. Elmer heard a scream, then saw the hawk slowly circle into the sky. He wished he could be up there, with a hawk's eyesight. He'd find Tangler for sure. He looked at his watch. Quarter after two. He'd have to run if he didn't want angry parents. He threw one more rock, high as he could. He didn't watch it fall.

There was the picnic in town. A dark drive home. A deep sleep.

II.

"Rise and shine!" his father called up the stairs. "We've got some errands to run."

Elmer was ready to pull the sheet over his head when he remembered the day before, and Tangler. He threw on his clothes and hustled to the breakfast table.

"Wash your face and comb the tangles out," said his mother, patting his sleep-mussed hair.

"No time," said Elmer. "Me and Dad've got to hurry."

"And where are you going?" she asked him.

"I don't know," he admitted. He was full of hope for this day, but he wanted his dad to say what they'd do. "Dad?" he asked.

"First we're going to find that old man. I believe his name is Crawshaw. We're going to tell him we don't have his horse. We'll drive over so we can look on the way. Then we're going to buy some fencing supplies. Might be Elmer here wouldn't mind helping if there was a reason for him to."

"You mean I might get a horse?"

"Someday, son," said his dad, "but you've got to be willing to do your part."

"Dear," said Elmer's mom, and she signaled Elmer's dad into their bedroom. They closed the door. It was one of their conferences. Usually, they just asked Elmer to go outside for a while. Even then he could sometimes hear loud voices, angry and sharp. Once, he'd gone clear out past the corral, to where a stand of trees began. But he still heard their voices, amazed by how far anger could travel.

This day, alone at the breakfast table, he overheard parts of what they said. His mother: "It's not fair unless you really plan to." His father: "But we have to be ready first." Then, later: "He has to earn it." Then his mother again: "Don't get his hopes up if we can't do it soon." His father: something about "next spring." Then his mother making a warning and his father saying "spoiled." His mother: "You're not getting your way?"

Elmer looked at his cereal when his mother came back into the kitchen and poured herself more coffee. She leaned against the counter. "Good things sometimes take a long time to happen," she said.

Elmer nodded. When his father came out of the bedroom, he left his cereal half-finished and followed, silently, to the truck.

Elmer put his head out the window and searched the passing countryside for Tangler. Nothing. A mile away his father slowed at a broken-down gate. "That's where he's been," said Elmer's dad. "Been and gone. Look at that fence." As they drove along it, the old barbed wire drooped, fell away broken from rusted staples. Posts, rotted in the ground, bent at every angle. "It'll take that old man more than a weekend to fix that," said Elmer's dad.

Elmer kept his eyes open. He saw everything else in the morning blue of sky, in the pale green of dusty grass, but not Tangler. And then they were finally at Crawshaw's.

The old man lived in an old shack of a house, as bent and crooked as he was, as brown with weather as the tobacco he chewed, as overgrown with weeds as his stubbly face.

"You knock on the door, son," Elmer's dad joked. "If I do, it'll probably fall in."

But the old man was suddenly at the door. He opened the screen, leaned out, and spat some tobacco juice into a rusty milk can on the porch. Then he limped out and sat noisily on an old sofa. The cushions were ripped. Elmer imagined it was full of a hundred mice, squeaking like the sofa's tired springs. "So, he ran away already," said the old man, his brown eyes gleaming. "I should've figured it. Jump a fence, did he?"

Elmer nodded, but the old man wasn't looking at him. Crawshaw was looking far away, as though he were watching Tangler gallop in a circle and jump.

"He jumped the gate," said Elmer's dad.

"Sure. Whatever." The old man brushed his arms. "You've got a magical horse, there," he said. He looked at Elmer. "He's little, like the Shetland in him, but he's strong and powerful like his Morgan blood. And you listen here. That little horse can do anything, if he has a mind to. Used to be in the circus, you know. He can count, climb a stepladder up and down, jump anything in front or beside him. He can do everything but cook your breakfast. Why, he can run so fast in one of them little bitty circus rings you couldn't see but just a blur. One old boy told me he could get going so fast he'd disappear. That what he did to you, boy?" The old man winked.

"Is Tangler really magical?" asked Elmer.

"Tangler?" asked the old man. "What do you mean, Tangler?"

"That's his name," said Elmer, excited. "I mean that's what I call him."

"Good name. He's tangled up my fence pretty good. You like him?"

"Sure," said Elmer. He looked at his dad, but his dad was looking away.

"He's yours if you want him, boy," Crawshaw said suddenly.

Elmer couldn't believe it. "Mine?" he asked.

"He's yours if you can catch him."

"Can we catch him, Dad?" Elmer asked.

"I don't know," said his father. "How did you catch him?" he asked Crawshaw.

92

"Oh, he knows me. After I bought him off the circus he was like a pet. That was before my wife died. Before my kids all moved to town. I'd catch him now, 'cept this rheumatism's got me so bad. I been laid up in the house ever since I was at your place yesterday."

"We'll think about it," said Elmer's dad. "Once we get our fence fixed."

Crawshaw threw his head back and laughed hard, his mouth open wide. His teeth were as black as rocks. He leaned forward. "You can't fence him in any more than you can fence in God's country air." He chuckled. "Get you some good feed and some sugar cubes. Treat him right. He'll come around. Especially to the boy here."

"We'll think about it," Elmer's dad said again, and he walked back toward the truck.

Elmer wondered if that meant no. These days, he couldn't quite tell what his dad was thinking, or just what his dad might do.

Elmer went and stood in front of the ratty sofa, close enough to fill his nose with the strong smell of the old man.

"Here's what you do," said Crawshaw. "You got to use color. Remember, he was in the circus. He likes bright colors. Put food color on the sugar cubes. Get you something really bright to wear, something bright as a clown costume. Oh, yeah, and if that don't work, there's one other thing. The little guy was raised on beer. He might still like a nip. That might do it." He smiled.

"Thanks," said Elmer. He jumped off the creaky old porch and ran to the truck.

"Good luck," called Crawshaw.

"We'll call you in a couple of days," Elmer's dad shouted back.

"No phone," yelled the old man through cupped hands.

Elmer's dad just nodded and backed the truck out of the dirt drive. It was a quiet ride home. When they reached their turnoff, Elmer's dad kept right on going, toward town.

"Where are we going?" asked Elmer.

"Where's your memory?" asked his dad.

"For fencing stuff?" Elmer asked, disappointed. "But he said that wouldn't matter. He said it wouldn't work. He told me how to catch Tangler."

"He told you a lot of things," said Elmer's dad. "And you believed it all.

Magic. Circuses. Disappearing. Elmer, you listen to me. A horse is a horse, and if you want to keep a horse you have to build a good fence. And if *you* want *this* horse, you have to help *me* mend fence."

"But we got to catch him. Soon," Elmer whined.

"We'll mend fence first, then try for the horse. And that's final. Do you understand?"

"Yes, sir," said Elmer. But he didn't want to wait very long. His horse would be wanting some sugar.

They went to town, came home, unloaded, ate, began work. Mending fence was slow. It made the day stretch longer and longer, like the barbed wire when they winched it at the corners. He didn't mean to, but Elmer kept pricking himself on the sharp barbs. "Pay attention," his dad would say. When Elmer put his fingers in his mouth, his dad told him to stop it.

His dad was hard to work with all through the long afternoon. They worked and worked, winched and winched, stretched and stretched, pounded and pounded the new staples into the old cedar posts. Elmer's dad pounded his thumb several times, each time letting out a big howl, and the last time throwing his hammer. They searched the tall pasture grass for ten minutes before Elmer found it. "Thanks," said his dad, standing next to Elmer and looking back at the fence. Even with the new staples and wire, the posts sagged. Between some posts, the old wire drooped more than before. Elmer wondered if his dad wanted him to say something. He felt his dad's hand on his shoulder. "It's not easy to do brand new things, is it?" his dad said.

"No, sir," said Elmer, and moved back to the fence. Tangler could jump it no problem no matter how well it was mended.

They strung two new wires before his dad let Elmer go back to the house. He was supposed to tell his mom they were done for the day, but when he walked by the back porch he saw her on a lawn chair, reading a book. He waved, and hurried inside. He had work to do, and fast. He ran into the kitchen with a chair and went for the top cabinet, where his mom kept the baking supplies.

The food coloring was right where he'd guessed, and he slipped the tiny red, blue, green, and yellow bottles into his back pockets. But the sugar cubes were not there. Surely they weren't all gone. He racked his brain, then remembered. One of the women his mother taught with had come to tea the month before. His mother had put the cubes into a little bowl, part of her best china set. He jumped off the chair and went to the china cupboard.

He'd just dug out a handful when he heard his mother open the back door. He slipped them in his shirt pocket, then put the lid on the bowl. "What are you doing?" asked his mom.

"Um . . . I thought I'd set the table for you. Dad says we're done for the day?"

"With my best china?" His mother smiled. Elmer could tell she knew he was up to something, but didn't want to challenge him.

"Well," he said, "it's kind of a special occasion. Since Mr. Crawshaw gave me Tangler."

"Elmer," said his mother, "you've still got to mend the fence, and then see if you can catch him. Your father thinks Mr. Crawshaw is just getting your hopes up. Don't get your heart too set, okay?"

"Okay," Elmer said. He stood up. His front shirt pocket bulged out, and he ran upstairs to unload the cubes. From his room he called down to her: "I'll come help you set the table in a second!"

"Thanks!" she yelled back.

At supper, his mom asked his dad how it was going with the fence.

"Okay," his dad said.

Elmer heard something in his dad's voice, but he couldn't tell what it was until his mom asked him the same question, and, just like his dad, he said, "Okay." The way they said it was exactly the same, like it wasn't really going okay. Usually his dad said things like he knew just what he thought and just what to do. That's what he'd always been like. But now there was something new in his dad's voice. Like doubt. Elmer liked that a little, but it scared him a little, too.

"Can I go outside?" he asked, when he'd finished everything but the green beans on his plate.

"Where to?" asked his dad.

"Just out," Elmer said. "Maybe take a long walk, then run home. Maybe my new school will have a cross-country team."

"Are you going horse hunting?" asked his dad. Elmer nodded. His father looked at the big kitchen clock. It was an old school clock Elmer's mom had brought home when the school where she taught had bought new ones. It always reminded Elmer of how he watched the clock at school, especially in the afternoon, waiting for the days to end. "You can go for a while. Be home by eight o'clock sharp." His father sounded very definite again.

Elmer bounded up the stairs to put on his running shoes. Then he found his school backpack. In it, he stuffed an old white shirt, some red pants he'd once worn in a school play, and a bright red hunting cap his dad had wanted to throw away. In the pack's zipper front, he slipped the sugar cubes and food coloring he'd snitched before dinner. Then, he hurried down the stairs and ran past the kitchen.

"What's in the pack?" he heard his mother ask.

"Just some stuff," he said, still running. He didn't hear his mother call him back, so he headed quickly away, toward the corral. He remembered seeing a big piece of rope hanging in one of the outbuildings. He creaked open the old door and there it was. He took it down. It was only about twelve feet long, and old and frayed, stiff and rough like Tangler's mane. But it was all he had, so he stuffed it in his pack, put the pack on his back, and took off at a slow jog.

An hour later, he was at Crawshaw's dirt drive, five miles from his house. He had a side stitch from running right after dinner, but he didn't care. He walked toward the house. The sun, lowering in the western sky, turned the horizon pale, then washed it lavender. Elmer was looking at the sky when he heard Crawshaw boom out: "Caught him yet, boy?"

"No," said Elmer, still breathing hard as he walked up to the porch.

"That tired and you ain't even started?"

Elmer sat on the edge of the porch. "I ran over here. I can't get any beer. My dad and mom never have any."

"So you thought I just might?" Crawshaw chuckled. "You might be right." Elmer looked at the old man, who spat a stream of tobacco juice, perfectly, into the milk can six feet from him. "And you might be wrong. You haven't tried the sugar and the colors, have you?"

Elmer was uncomfortable. He hoped Crawshaw would help him, but it was just questions, like being at home. So he stood up and took off his backpack.

"You think I'll be able to catch him?" Elmer asked, pulling out the old rope.

"Wait a minute, son," said the old man. "You go near him with that rope he'll be halfway to Timbuktu before you can say Jack Robinson."

"But you brought him to our place with a rope."

"And how well did that work?" asked the old man.

"Not very, I guess," admitted Elmer.

"But he couldn't have stayed at all without it," Crawshaw said. "And I wanted him to stay. I ain't got time for him anymore. Seems to me like you might. Once you catch him, that is. Once you get him used to you. But you can't do it with a rope."

Elmer dropped the rope and began emptying the rest of the pack. "Good," said the old man when he showed him the pants and shirt and hat. "Great," he said when Elmer showed him the food coloring and the sugar cubes.

"How'd you know I wanted a horse?" Elmer asked.

"You know a boy who don't? Now, you get those cubes colored. Get your clothes on. It's getting late."

Elmer looked at his watch. Half past six. He opened the bottles of food coloring and watched the drops of liquid soak into the cubes. He colored each cube. He made one of all the colors, a different color on each side. Then he laid the white shirt onto the porch and made long stripes of colors top to bottom like a rainbow of suspenders. He let the shirt dry while he put on the bright red pants over his jogging shorts. "Good," said the old man, when Elmer finally put on the shirt and bright hunting cap, completing his costume. "Now, skedaddle. If you don't see him tonight, we'll think about the beer tomorrow. Can you get away?"

"I will," Elmer promised. "I think Dad'll let me. But I don't think he likes Tangler. He doesn't believe what you said about circuses and all."

"What about you? Do you believe it, boy?" asked Crawshaw.

"Yes," said Elmer. He turned away, then back around. "Thanks, Mr. Crawshaw," he said. "Thanks a lot."

"Call me by my first name," said the old man, "if we're going to be friends."

"What is your first name?" Elmer asked.

"You know it, I'll bet," said Crawshaw. "Guess."

"I don't know."

"Elmer," said the old man.

"What?" asked Elmer.

Crawshaw just laughed. "Elmer Crawshaw. That's my name."

"Really?" asked Elmer. "That's my name, too."

"Elmer Crawshaw?" joked the old man.

"No. Elmer D. Peterson."

"Well, I'm mighty pleased to meet you, Elmer," said Elmer. "It ain't every day you find another Elmer, is it?"

"No, sir."

"Elmer."

"Right. No, sir, Elmer."

"Now get that horse, boy." Elmer Crawshaw shooed Elmer D. Peterson away.

At first, Elmer felt weird running in the long red pants, the funny shirt and hat, the sugar cubes crunching in his hands like decaying dice. But he wanted to find Tangler, and he ran a mile, fast, before he ducked under a fence and started through some pasture near where he remembered seeing Tangler the day before. He tried to stay in the high places, where Tangler could see him and be attracted to the colors. He trotted into the dusk, feeling good about Elmer Crawshaw, that anyone in the world would have the same first name he did. The old man had known he wanted a horse. Elmer Crawshaw wanted him to catch Tangler. He would help. He would be a friend.

Elmer heard a whinnying and stopped. He turned a full circle, but saw nothing. Then he heard it again, behind him. He saw Tangler come out of a draw, and Elmer danced, waving his arms like a clown might. Then he held out a handful of sugar cubes. "Come here, boy," he called. "Come here." And Tangler came. Elmer couldn't believe it.

Ten feet away, Tangler stopped, thrust his neck out, his nose forward, and sniffed. Elmer extended his arm as far as he could without taking a step. Tangler stretched forward, too, then took several small steps. Elmer tiptoed closer until, finally, Tangler brushed Elmer's extended palm. He snuffed through his nose, then his tongue came out, singled out the cube of many colors, and brought it into his mouth. Tangler crunched the cube. "Good boy," said Elmer. "Good boy."

He didn't know what to do next, but he knew it was late, and he knew he'd have to use the few other colored sugar cubes to lead Tangler home. So he did what he didn't want to do. He turned and walked away, toward his house. In twenty feet he looked back. Tangler was following him. Elmer stopped and fed the horse another cube. Then he walked some more. Two cubes later they were at the fence. Elmer took a chance. He slid under and stood on the road, holding out a sugar cube. Tangler neared the fence, looked over it, whinnied, and promptly jumped it. Elmer couldn't believe his eyes. He gave Tangler another cube, his next to last one, then ran down the road, Tangler following along behind.

A half-mile from his house, Elmer fed Tangler his last cube. He began trotting again. It was getting very late, already well after eight o'clock. He'd be in big trouble if he didn't get home soon. He heard Tangler behind him, and ran faster.

Then he couldn't hear anything but his own footfalls. He stopped and turned around. He couldn't see anything but lumpy shadows on the distant road. "Tangler!" he called. Nothing answered. He stood quietly, disappointed.

"Elmer!" It was his father's voice. He took out running toward it. Right as he neared his lane, he thought he heard something. He stopped one last time. That's when he saw it. A shadow galloped toward him. Hooves sounded the gravel like hollow bones. Tangler was coming right at him, and Elmer froze. He wanted to close his eyes, but he wanted to see what Tangler would do. Elmer squeezed his hands together as hard as he could. His face winced. Tangler thundered right up to him, then leaped, clearing Elmer's head with a rush of wind. The horse landed without breaking stride, leaving behind only the soft leathery smell of his hide. Tangler raced away, down the road.

"Elmer!" his father shouted again.

"Coming," Elmer said. He quickly stripped off his clown costume and stuffed it back in his pack. Then, he ran up the lane, his breath still short with excitement. He explained everything to his dad, but he was very late. His father claimed he hadn't heard the horse run up and jump over Elmer. His father was mad, and grounded him for the rest of the week.

III

Elmer woke to the sound of his father's boots on the attic stairs. "You can work with me, or you can stay inside. That's it." His dad was still mad.

"Inside," Elmer said. Then, "I really did see him. He really did follow me home and eat sugar cubes out of my hand. He really did jump over me."

"Elmer," said his dad. "I want to believe you. But I also have to punish you for staying out way past when I told you to be in."

"It was like a job, Dad," Elmer said. "I just wanted to finish it. You come in late to dinner sometimes when you have to finish something."

"And you can, too, when you're an adult." His father looked at him but Elmer turned away. "Your mother's gone to town. But she'll be back by lunch. You help her around the house today. You understand?"

"What are you going to do?" Elmer asked.

"Mend fence, of course. First things first, Elmer."

"He can jump it, anyway."

"We'll see." His father went back down the stairs. Just before he went outside he stuck his head into the stairwell. "You just keep from getting sassy. You understand? You don't know everything."

Neither do you, Elmer thought. He wanted his dad to believe him, to understand. "Yes, sir," was all he said. He went to the window and watched his father walk through the gate, past the corral, toward the back pasture.

As soon as he couldn't see his dad anymore, he hurried to his closet. He had made up his mind the night before, when his dad didn't believe his story. He would sneak out, run to Crawshaw's shack, pick up the beer, and get Tangler to come with him.

Off he ran, pack on his back. This time, he found a shortcut, through different pastures, to the old man's house. "Morning, Elmer," said Crawshaw from the sofa on the porch.

"Morning, Elmer," Elmer said back. He sat down on the edge of the porch and told his friend all about the night before.

"Atta boy," said Crawshaw when he heard Elmer's story. "Sounds like he likes you."

"I don't have any more sugar cubes."

"That's okay. 'Cause I found a bottle of beer. Now get on your costume. He'll be somewhere between here and your place, if I know him."

Elmer threw on his clothes, emptying the backpack. Crawshaw reached behind the sofa, then stood up, twisting the top off a brown bottle of Budweiser. He also had several old sponges, brownish purple like big pieces of liver. He picked up Elmer's pack, stuffed it full of sponges, and poured in the whole bottle of beer. A little foam came up to the top, but Crawshaw zipped it shut.

"Well," he said, throwing the empty bottle at a fifty-five-gallon drum he used for trash, "now he'll follow you anywhere, once he gets a whiff."

"Thanks," said Elmer. He put on the pack. It leaked a little onto his shirt and pants. "I'm not supposed to be out today."

"You get in trouble last night?" Crawshaw didn't wait for an answer. "Tell me, you all have any tack?" Elmer looked puzzled.

"Bridle. Saddle. Halter. Stuff like that," Crawshaw explained.

"No, sir."

"Well, get going," Crawshaw said. "You get that horse home. Good luck."

"Thanks, Elmer," said Elmer, and he ran off. He could feel the beer in his pack slosh around. His pants were getting soaked. The warm beer smelled a little like bread dough and a little like rotting apples.

Elmer tried to go in a straight line between Crawshaw's house and his. He ran across country he'd never seen before, and everywhere he looked he saw new things: the way the trees bent from the steady winds, the way the rock faces mirrored each other from one rise to the next, the way the grass turned blue along its edges, the way the ponds reflected the sky. Maybe it was because he was grounded and wasn't supposed to be out. Maybe it was because since Tangler he'd been exploring the countryside so much. Maybe it was because he wanted to see Tangler in each new view, so he looked close. But he loved being out in the beautiful countryside, nothing but grass beneath him, sky over him, and the whispering wind pushing and pulling him along. He wished he never had to go home.

He went down a draw, crossed a dried-up old creek bed, and began climbing up a rise. A little ways up he jumped over a thin wire. He hadn't seen anything quite like it before, but he was pretty sure it was electrified. He almost touched it, then decided he'd better not. Near the top of the rise, he stopped and looked all around him. He saw three things at once. Above him, farther up the rise, he saw a huge cow, black and stocky, thick in the shoulders and neck. Its eyes glinted in the sun. Just as Elmer realized it was not a cow, but a bull, he saw Tangler, behind the animal, past another thin wire and another fence line. Then, to his right, he saw a plume of dust rising from the gravel road. A truck, his father's truck, came over the rise.

Elmer stood very still. There was no use running. Either his father would see him in the crazy clown costume or he wouldn't. But before he could tell anything about his dad, Elmer heard a huge bellow. The great black bull tossed its head. Then it pawed the ground and bellowed again. Elmer changed his mind about running. He tried to judge which fence line in the treeless pasture was closest. The bull lowered its massive head.

Then Tangler whinnied. The bull looked behind him, distracted for a second by Tangler. Elmer took advantage of the moment, running toward the road, away from the bull and away from Tangler. That's when he saw his father's truck stop. He was running straight for it, his legs pumping, the beer on his back churning to foam.

Even as he ran, Elmer thought of all the trouble he was in. For just a moment, he felt mad. Mad at the bull, mad at his dad, mad at Elmer Crawshaw, mad at Tangler. He wondered why all this had to happen to him, Elmer D. Peterson. Then he couldn't think anymore, because he could hear the bull's heavy footsteps. He looked back, over his shoulder, still running, and everything seemed slow motion. The bull was lumbering toward him. Tangler whinnied, reared back, shook his head. "Tangler!" Elmer shouted. Then, because he wasn't watching where he was going, he tripped on a clump of bluestem and went down flat on his face.

"Elmer!" his dad yelled. He looked up.

"Dad!" he screamed back. His father began to climb the fence.

Then Elmer heard a loud whinnying, almost a whine, and he sat up. Tangler jumped the fence and raced toward the bull, who was halfway to where

Elmer sat. Elmer stood up, but he couldn't run. Like the night before, he could only watch what Tangler would do. He was afraid, but fascinated. Tangler galloped across the pasture, gaining on the bull.

"Elmer! Run, Elmer!" his dad yelled again, over the fence now and looking for something to throw at the bull.

But Elmer couldn't move. He was frozen to the spot.

"Elmer!" It was his mother's voice this time. Elmer hadn't seen her in the truck with his dad. He waved to her, just like everything was fine, just like there was no bull running toward him, just like he didn't have on a silly clown costume, just like he didn't have a backpack full of beer-soaked sponges leaking all over him.

He could feel the earth shaking with the pounding of the bull's hooves. He looked right at the bull now. It was huge. Tangler was just behind it, though, tail up, galloping faster than Elmer had ever seen him run. And then, when the bull was just thirty feet from Elmer, Tangler caught up to the charging animal. Elmer couldn't see what happened, but suddenly the bull crumpled onto its front legs, bellowing. The bull looked all around. Tangler danced away, distracting the bull from Elmer. There was something in Tangler's mouth. Elmer felt a hand on his shoulder, tugging at him. It was his dad.

"Look," said Elmer, pointing. They both looked, amazed. Tangler had bit the bull's tail clear off, and he tossed it in his mouth like a whip. The bull stood back up and stared at Elmer and his dad. It stared at Tangler. It let out a huge bellow, then started after the horse. Tangler galloped away, turning a circle, confusing the bull.

"C'mon," Elmer's dad said, and he and Elmer backed away, their eyes on the bull, and Tangler. They hopped the electric wire, then climbed the fence, all the time watching Tangler run the bull. Elmer's mother came over and stood beside them. Tangler was amazing, running in circles, turning the bull every which way. Once, when the bull charged him, Tangler made a tight circle and jumped right over the enraged animal. Elmer couldn't believe how fast, how nimble Tangler was, his nostrils flaring, the bull's tail still whipping from his teeth. Finally, after five minutes of bull baiting, Tangler had the huge animal so tired, so dizzy, so confused, that it crumpled again onto the grass, its head lazily following Tangler's movements as though it was drunk.

"Greatest show on earth, ain't it?" Elmer Crawshaw walked up behind them. He had parked his truck down the road a ways, earlier, when they were all too busy and anxious to notice him. Crawshaw lifted the pack off Elmer's back. "Thanks for helping me, son," he said. He began walking away with the pack. When he neared his truck, he turned around and yelled back at them. "I know I shouldn't have told you to come over. But I couldn't have done it without you. I've got your pay in my truck there." He walked a ways toward his pickup and threw Elmer's pack into the back. Elmer and his mother and father followed the old man.

Then Tangler whinnied, and, free from the bull, he trotted toward the road. He jumped the little electric wire, then jumped the fence line thirty feet from them. He started toward them, but halfway, as though remembering something, Tangler trotted up to the fence and with a shake of his head he tossed the bull's tail into the pasture. Then he turned and trotted toward them, his nostrils still flared. Before they could wonder what he'd do next, he passed them and jumped up into Crawshaw's pickup, just like a dog would do. Elmer and his dad and mom hurried to the truck.

Tangler was nuzzling Elmer's pack. Crawshaw reached in, unzipped it for him, and Tangler nuzzled in and pulled a sponge out with his teeth. They could hear him sucking up the beer.

"Elmer," said Crawshaw. "You ride in the back with Tangler here. You can inspect the tack there. It's your payment for helping. Peterson, you can ride up with me. The missus can drive your truck home." Crawshaw spoke with quick authority. Elmer's dad nodded. So did his mom. It was like a dream that couldn't be happening. Elmer jumped up next to Tangler and pulled another sponge from the pack. He petted Tangler and put his face in the horse's strong neck.

Then they started out, toward home, Elmer Crawshaw and Elmer's dad in the truck cab. Elmer D. Peterson and Tangler, along with a bridle, saddle, halter, and lead ropes, were the cargo. Elmer's mom followed a ways behind, giving their dust time to blow away. Elmer waved at her once, and she waved back, smiling and shaking her head.

He didn't know what kind of trouble he was in. Maybe pretty bad. He saw Crawshaw and his dad talking. They didn't seem to be mad, but he didn't know what his dad might be thinking. Still, all the way home, all he could think about was Tangler. He was right next to the horse. His horse. Tangler liked him. Tangler would get used to him. No matter what happened to him, he knew he'd have a friend. Two friends, because there was Elmer Crawshaw, too. He thought about that all the way home. He realized he might as well feel good about his life for as long as he could.

When Crawshaw turned into their lane, Elmer's spirits sank. Crawshaw stopped his truck near the corral gate. Elmer saw Crawshaw say one more thing to his dad, then the two men climbed out. Elmer's mom pulled up nearby. Elmer grabbed another sponge out of his pack for Tangler. Then he waited for his dad to say something. They all gathered around the truck.

Finally, Elmer's dad cleared his throat. "Son," he said, "I guess he's yours. You caught him, just like the man said. Or maybe he caught you. He's one heck of a horse."

"The greatest ever," said Elmer. He didn't know whether he should say "I'm sorry" or "Thank you." He just stood next to Tangler, his clown costume itching like crazy.

Midlin, Kansas, Jump Shot

Approach any central Kansas town and you see the grain elevator, water tower, church steeple, the vaulting county courthouse: anything trying to find sky. Say you're traveling west on Highway 52, toward Midlin, population 2,789, Home of the Midlin Lions. Farthest south in your gaze, just above the green fuzz of elm trees – carefully planted and watered in the last century – is the cylindrical landmark of the Farmer's Co-op and Magnusen's Mill and Elevator. Then, as though marching toward the highway to intersect your drive, the flag-mounted cupola of the Chichkawh County Courthouse, the Midlin Water Tower, and the bell tower and steeple of the St. Cloud Church.

If you are Ken Johnson, you might remember your first climb into the cabin of Magnusen's Elevator, how dizzy with heat and height you felt, how frightened you were to look down, but how, when you did, and studied Midlin, you could see yourself in all the comings and goings of your life. You saw the home you were born into. The school where you played basketball, the star of a team in a long line of teams expected to win. The Greyhound Depot where you left and returned from your first trip away by yourself. The Chichkawh River Bridge. The ripple of land where the Chichkawh joins the Blue. But you don't like to think about the Blue River.

Ken Johnson will also remember the story his father has told him, of how, when the Midlin Water Tower was built in 1928, when *he* was a boy, his gang challenged him to climb its steel-grid ladder all the way to the top and leave his initials. He did, though none of his friends were ever bold enough to climb far enough to check. When Ken climbed it, in his sixteenth year, he found not only his father's initials but the initials of his mother. Then, Ken put his finger over his own name to trace its letters, which his father had also etched into the steel along with the names of Ken's sisters. Ken wondered which was more bold, to climb great heights on a dare, or to imagine and name a future so clearly – and to be right.

In his senior year, the week before school, Ken played ball every day with the Lions in the sweltering gymnasium of the Borsten Consolidated School. The school halls are lined with framed class pictures. Ken didn't have to look anymore to feel the eyes of his mother and father, class of '37, or the eyes of his uncles and aunts, grandparents and cousins. Someday, he'd have a place on the wall in the hall, staring at hapless students, who would wonder why he kept his crew cut when everyone else in his class was letting their hair grow, or why they'd never seen a picture of him in which he smiled. His sister Meg called him "Lemon." Ken called her "Nutmeg."

Ken's other sister, Kate, is the reason his basketball game became so intense in his junior year: Ken said her name like a magic chant; he took all his grief and anger and focused it into his eyes and hands; he concentrated until everything left him but her name and the game. She drowned in the Blue River. She was trying to hide along the bank late one evening in the summer of 1955. The Conway Island side was always eaten away by water, and the roots were loose. Among them, Kate's feet had lost their hold. She grabbed wildly at the crumbling soil, then tumbled into the water. Ken saw her go under. And during the year after Kate's death, Ken watched his mother almost go under, too, facing the emptiness of a bedroom, a closet full of sleeves waiting for arms.

From the time he was three years old, he had slept with a basketball on his bed, always. He loved the game, wondered if *it* might take him away, into his life. He knew basketball: you bounce the ball and it comes back to you; you miss a shot and you have another chance; you make a shot and you knew it was going in all along; you play within boundaries, against a clock, but you can try anything. And there's always the next game. Nothing else in Ken's life had been so predictable, yet so free, as basketball.

Ken's father taught him the jump shot. He was maybe eight years old, and most of the kids at school were still throwing sissy free throws, the ball cupped in their palms and held between their legs. Ken held the ball at his chest, and when he looked over it, he could see the rim, the target, his goal. He stood flat-footed, moving only his knees and wrists, and he could shoot seven out of ten already. His father watched him from the window of their living room and knew it was time for the jump.

By the end of the summer, Ken had perfected the fade-away jump. Ken walked and ran all over Midlin with his basketball, sometimes making it through a whole day without losing the dribble.

"You can hear that boy coming and going," Mr. Holmberg once told Ken's mother. "He's the only one can come into the Supply Company, buy a pound of tenpenny nails, pay up, take his change and get out the door, all the time dribbling that infernal ball."

In 1956 Ken was more than twice as old as that dribbling boy. He was ready to start his senior year. The preseason, pre-school-year practices at the gymnasium went well. Coach Wellburn said they had a good chance to go to Regionals, maybe even State. Ken wondered if life was like basketball: the better you were, the farther from home you went to play, or work, or make a life for yourself. And could you ever get so far away that there was no place to return to, victorious or defeated?

After Kate's death, and sometimes before that, Ken thought of his parents as defeated. They had everything anyone really wanted or needed: his father's good job managing Midlin's Palace Theater, their new Hudson car, television, a nice house with a garage, kids who did well in school. But Ken's mother always seemed on the verge of something: tears or tirades, Ken couldn't tell. And Ken never really heard his father talk about his life.

Ken sometimes went to the Chichkawh Bridge late at night, and stared down into the darkness of night-time water. Mr. James, one of his math teachers, had made the class study bridge construction. Ken wondered what it would be like to have a suspension bridge across the Blue, to have cable above you so that you didn't feel the massive weight that held you up. He wondered if it would feel like the jump shot, a suspension of a different kind, in which you did everything in your power to get yourself up, and then, just when you couldn't stay up any longer, you put a ball in the air and watched it rise on its arc until it couldn't stay up any longer, and then you landed on solid floor and hoped the ball did, too, with only the sounds of tennis shoes hitting wood and leather hitting string with a "swish." There was that moment, though, when everything was possible. And then everything was as it was: a made shot or a missed one. Kate must have had such a moment, past which everything became what it was: every drowning or dying person must have just such a moment.

"Do you sometimes wonder what it'd be like to live somewhere else?" Ken asked his mother around that time.

"Midlin born, Midlin bred," his mother said, repeating something Ken had heard so often that he used to chant to himself, "Midlin bored, Midlin dead."

"Didn't you ever want to go anywhere else?" Ken asked.

"Your father was here," she said.

"But what about you?"

"I like it here," she said. She smiled and ruffled his hair, as she had when he was smaller.

"Even since Kate?" he asked.

"You're curious all of a sudden," she said. She never said Kate's name anymore.

Ken said nothing.

"Your life is with you wherever you go," his mother said, finally.

Ken knew what his mother was saying. As he walked Midlin during what he thought would be his last summer there, he speculated that his life was like a jump shot. His father had told him that the key to the jump shot was not in the shot, but in the preparation. "Most shots fail just as the player plants his feet," said his father. "If he doesn't have the footing, he might as well throw the ball away.

"Because nothing is solid. There's no good lift, no falling away, no sureness."

Coach said the same thing over and over again: "Fundamentals. Fundamentals. Fundamentals."

Midlin was fundamental. Ken sensed that wherever he went. "Down to earth," people called themselves, but Ken was someone who had defined himself by his ability to get off the earth, higher than anyone else, at least long enough to get the ball through the hoop.

"Don't people want something else?" he asked his mother.

"No," she said. "Most people want what they have. At least until they have hard times."

"You've had hard times," Ken said.

Ken's mother swiped at her hair as he'd seen her do a hundred times since Kate's death: hands through bangs, then combing along the temples, then patting the sides. This was her way of hiding a quick flash of tears. "Would it be any different anywhere else?" she asked.

Ken knew she did not expect an answer. He'd already learned that most people didn't, at least not to the hard questions. He remembered Kate's funeral. He could think only one thought: *I should have saved her.* A month later, he climbed the stairs to Dr. Medford Dreadlock's Health Clinic.

The doctor was in his office, playing checkers. Whenever he wasn't with a patient, he put the board in the middle of the examination table and moved from one side to the other, playing against himself, examining the checker moves with the same concentration as when he listened to an old man's palpitating heart. "You want to take the next move?" the doctor asked.

"No, sir," said Ken.

"Then I'll do it." Dreadlock had set up a quadruple jump. "A lot of jumps," said the doctor. "But not a jump shot. How's your game?"

"Okay," said Ken.

Dreadlock lifted the board carefully and set it on his desk. He patted his exam table.

"Something wrong with *you*?" asked Dreadlock. "Or something wrong with the world?"

Ken forced himself into the air, though he knew he'd never get the ball released. "I keep thinking . . . I keep wondering . . . I mean, about Kate."

"I had to pronounce her dead," said the doctor. "Of course she *was* dead. But I had to try to listen for her heart one more time. And then sign the papers."

"I could have saved her, maybe," Ken said to the floor. He couldn't quit thinking about Kate, her limp body dragged onto the bank of the Blue River, her mouth running with muddy water, her clothes already seeming to melt into the clay.

"If you could have saved her, it would have happened. It's that simple. I have to believe that. Because a lot of things happen to a doctor. I think you have to believe it, too."

"Maybe if . . ."

"'Maybe' and 'If' are words for philosophers and for the guilty. You're not guilty, Ken. But maybe you're a philosopher?"

"I don't think so."

"When you came in here," said the doctor, "I was just ready to make that quadruple jump. In checkers you have to jump if you *have* a jump. I took it because I had to. If you had taken the move, you would have had to jump, the same as me. Who was trapped, me or you?"

"I don't know."

"In checkers, it's always the game that wins, as long as we keep playing it. And that shouldn't make us mad. It'd be silly to feel beaten by a checkerboard."

"Yeah."

"Well, it's silly to feel defeated by life." Dreadlock swept the checkers off the board and handed it to Ken. "Keep this," he said, "to remember our talk."

Ken had kept each basketball he'd ever owned. They sat on the shelf in his bedroom, then on a shelf in the garage. He saved them not because he thought he might need them. He saved them the same way his sisters had saved their dolls: they didn't play with them much anymore, but each one contained an accumulated affection that made it hard to just toss away.

After Kate's death, all of her things, stored in her sanctuary of a room, became an accumulation not of affection, but of grief. Ken's father kept suggesting that they box most of her belongings and give them away, maybe to a needy family, maybe in another town. Ken's mother refused, saying simply, "I can't." But the tension in the house rose, until Ken heard his parents behind the closed door of Kate's room one day, his father saying, "For God's sake, there's no reason to keep her underwear, is there?" And his mother's shrill voice keening, "It was *hers.*"

The next day Ken went to the Palace Theater for an old piece of canvas curtain. He waited until an evening when his father left for work at the Palace and his mother forced herself out to choir practice. He was supposed to watch Meg, so he recruited her. "Go put on really dark clothes," he told her.

"How come?" she asked.

"Because that way nobody will see us."

"That canvas is big and white," she said.

Ken thought about that. "I just don't want them to see *us.*"

She shrugged her shoulders, left the room, and returned wearing what he wore: denim jeans and shirt. They went to the garage and filled the canvas with all of Ken's old basketballs. And off they went, dragging the bulging canvas through the garage door and heading down through the alley toward town.

"Why are you doing this?" asked Meg, when they could see the single light on top of the courthouse.

"I don't know," Ken admitted. As he'd put them in the canvas, he'd counted sixteen basketballs, almost one for each year of his life. Maybe if he put them somewhere public, he could remember them better. Maybe they would mean more. He could get rid of them, but they wouldn't be gone. "Why does Virgil Straten keep every car he's ever owned lined up behind his gas station?"

"People are weird," said Meg. "And so are you."

They reached the alley behind Midlin City Hall and went for the corner between the parking lot and the flat-roofed, one-story building. One after the next, Ken hurled the balls onto the roof, listened to them land flatly on the thick tar. Once, Ken and Meg had to flatten themselves against the building when the sheriff's car cruised by to park at the courthouse.

"They're going to know these are yours," Meg said. "When they find them."

"I know that," said Ken.

Ken imagined the sixteen balls, swimming in spring rain, stinking in the summer heat, their skins drying and curling, then flaking off in the fall like so many leaves, freezing like rocks in the winter. "In a town like ours, everybody finds out everything eventually. But it's *when* they find out. That's what I want to see."

"Let's go home," said Meg.

"I've got to take this by the P. We'll go in through the back and throw it behind the stage." Ken wadded the canvas under his arm.

The Palace was lit so that anyone in town could head for its glow. Except for the single floodlight on the courthouse cupola, the Palace was the last and brightest light to stay on in Midlin. When Ken and Meg sneaked through the back door, they heard bazooka fire, bombs bursting through the Palace speakers, the rapid fire of machine guns. "Get down," they heard a voice, "they see us now."

Ken had sat with his father and previewed *The Longest Day*, with its all-star Hollywood cast, its reenaction of the bravery and daring of D-day. "Mostly a crock," said his dad at the end. "But they sure make it look good."

Ken hurled the canvas into a storeroom as though it were a grenade, and he and Meg raced home. On the way, he thought of his basketballs, sprouted on the Midlin City Hall roof like mushrooms after a rainstorm, and, like everything else in Midlin, waiting to be discovered.

Ken remembered the day he found out the balls had been discovered. He was walking home late at night, after practicing by himself in the Borsten School gym. State Championship was just a week away. He'd let his shooting percentage dip below 60 percent in the last couple of games, and "Practice," as his father always reminded him, "makes perfect."

Just as Ken reached Myrah Street, Sheriff Sam Poplar pulled up beside him and rolled down his window. "Cold night," said the sheriff.

"Yeah," said Ken.

"Want a ride?"

"I get hot practicing. I need to cool off."

"Courthouse janitor says some basketballs are cooling off on the roof of City Hall. Saw 'em from the tower."

Ken nodded, trying not to smile.

"Don't suppose they're causing anybody any trouble up there," said Sheriff Poplar. "Not really."

"Nope," said Ken. He hadn't figured he'd get into trouble. "Nobody at home saw they were gone," he said.

"Win State and those balls might be worth something someday. Souvenirs."

"I don't like souvenirs," said Ken.

"But you didn't throw them away, did you?" said the sheriff.

"Are you going to tell anyone?" asked Ken.

"Nope," said the sheriff. He revved the engine and started to roll up his window. But he didn't pull away. Through a crack in the window, he said, "Kids like to leave their mark. Natural as a dog on a hydrant. Just don't go scratching your name into the water tower." Then off he went.

On the day before Ken left for college, he climbed the water tower to look down again, one last time, on Midlin. His basketballs were still on the City Hall roof, graying like his parents' hair, collecting dust like the museum of Kate's room, slowly flattening, like everything in Midlin seemed to do.

The Lions had not won State. Ken stole the ball from Winfield with ten seconds left on the clock. The Lions were only a point behind. Ken began looking for picks. Nine. *Kate, Kate, Kate.* He found one, right side, his own center, right where he should be. Eight. He dribbled along the foul line, losing his man to the impact with his center. Seven. Another opponent came up on him, a little too fast, so Ken hesitated, faked stopping the dribble, and the kid fell down. Six. *Kate, Kate, Kate.* Ken went up, high, and saw the rim. Five. Ken released the ball and watched its arc, saying to himself, *Kate, Kate, Kate.* Four. The ball hit the back of the rim and bounced straight up. Three. *Kate, Kate, Kate,* and the ball started back down, and Ken came down, landed solid, prepared for a rebound, should there be one. Two. And the ball hit the front of the rim and bounced, away, but toward Ken, as though doing the jump shot in reverse. One. And Ken went up for the ball, met it with his hands, tried to shoot again, but heard the buzzer. No time left, though the ball didn't know that, and it continued toward the basket and through, a perfect swish before pandemonium and congratulations.

But Ken watched the referees huddle. He knew what they would say. His hands knew. His body knew. He was still holding the ball when the buzzer sounded. He had lost the game. And so it was. "A tenth of a second," he told his father. "I should have got that last shot off sooner."

"No," said his father. "You should have made the first one sooner. You didn't need that little fake. Your fall-away jump shot has that already."

The next day Ken went to visit the cemetery, to find Kate's grave. For the first time, he thought, he had an inkling of what his parents felt. Kate was dead. Her name, said over and over in his mind, playing basketball, was not enough, just as her name, etched by his father in the metal of the water tower, had not been enough. "I'm sorry," he said aloud. Twice now he had failed her. He had failed his town. He left the cemetery and walked home along Main Street.

Bus

The sign said "Bus Stop" and sure enough the bus stopped there, though Michael would be the first to say it never stopped at the same time. In fact, he hoped it never would. If it ever did, he couldn't shift his bag, look at his watch, climb the stairs and say to the driver – Evelyn on this day, a Monday – "Never the same time, never," and take his seat as close to the front as he could.

He had one of those digital watches, sold for almost nothing at Wal-Mart, but it was exact: hour, minute, second. The stopwatch even had tenths of seconds: Michael's head spun when he watched time go by that fast. Since it was Monday, Michael would get off downtown, at Tenth and Kansas. Evelyn knew that, but when he said, "I'm working this morning. At the Express," she said, "Is that right? Working hard, or hardly working."

He loved it when Evelyn said that. Michael beamed at his reflection in the bus window. "Working hard," he said. "Working very hard."

Evelyn was better than Frank. When Frank drove the route, he jerked the bus through the corners and loved to honk the horn to warn people he was making the wide turns. Michael had a theory: Frank was skinny, "Thinner than a mouse's tail," Michael's mother would have said. And so Frank had to make something large of everything. If he weren't driving a bus he'd be knocking down buildings for a living. But Evelyn, she was already large. She was very large. Her bus driver's cap looked like a little beanie on her big head. So she knew about big, and the bus just moved as smoothly as she did. Evelyn, Michael thought, knew what to do with size.

A month ago, Michael had tried to tell her about that. "*You* know how to move. And how to move that big bus. Big, right?"

She hadn't said a word, but she sure sped off the minute his foot hit the pavement. The next day, she didn't say "hardly working," and Michael stared out the window. He counted the poles as they went by. And not just the telephone poles. He was counting street lamp poles, traffic light poles, street sign poles, any old fence pole. He could hardly keep up, like when the time moved by so fast on his watch. Even when he shut his eyes he had seen shapes squiggling past.

"I'm cooking today," he told Evelyn. He always sat right behind her. "It's Monday, so I'm cooking the soups."

She nodded.

"'Home-cooked soups,' like the sign in front of the Express says."

"But you're not home," she told him.

Michael couldn't figure that one out. They did call them "home-cooked soups," but they were cooked at the restaurant. Michael cooked them like he did the ones at home. But he wasn't home, just like Evelyn said.

Alphabet was his favorite at home, but Mr. Sandori at the Express wouldn't let him cook alphabet soup. Michael liked the words he saw while he stirred. The letters boiled up and then went under again, but sometimes, in just a little instant, he could read something. It was like being spoken to. And then he realized he *was* being spoken to.

"What?" he asked Evelyn.

She examined him in the rearview mirror, her eyes small in the doughy cheeks of her face. "I said, 'What're you cooking today?' Anything worth eating?"

"Soup day," said Michael. "Home-cooked soups."

"But *what* soups?" asked Evelyn.

"Don't know," said Michael.

"I thought you were cooking today."

"I always cook the soups on Monday. Hard work. All morning I cook the soups. Fridays, too."

"So what're you going to cook? Me, I drive a bus. I go to work, I know what my route's going to be. I don't just make it up, you know. I'd get fired."

"Mr. Sandori won't fire me," said Michael. "I work hard. Mr. Sandori goes to the supermarket, early, before it's even open. He sees what the people didn't buy over the weekend. Whatever it is, I make it into a soup."

"What if they didn't buy lettuce?" asked Evelyn. "You making lettuce soup today?"

Michael blushed. "Nobody would eat lettuce soup."

"They don't buy eggs, you make egg drop soup?"

"We don't have that," said Michael.

Evelyn pulled gently to the side of the street and stopped the bus for the man and woman who would get off at the State Hospital. They were orderlies, Michael had heard. But their patients weren't orderly. He wondered if that's why they called them orderlies, like maybe it would rub off. Michael's mother sometimes took him places, like concerts and plays and museums, and she always said maybe something would rub off on him.

"You know what I wish?" said Michael once the orderlies sat down and Evelyn was speeding down the street. "I wish they couldn't sell alphabet noodles. Then Mr. Sandori could buy a bunch of them, and I could make alphabet soup. That's my real home-cooked soup, cause I cook it at home."

"I thought people who cooked for a living hated cooking at home," said Evelyn.

"I like to cook alphabet soup," said Michael.

"You think I like to drive after work?" asked Evelyn. "You think I'm crazy?"

"My mother says my cat is crazy, because he eats alphabet soup, too," said Michael.

"I can see it, you feeding the cat the alphabet. That's a good one."

Michael turned to look out the window. Evelyn was sounding funny again, and he knew just to leave her alone. He started to play his number game, the multiplication trick. He would count something: cars, windows in nearby houses, doors of buildings, and, as fast as he could, multiply them by all the numbers from one to ten. He could do it as fast as he could whisper it: especially with two and nine and five. Those were the easy ones. With the twos, Michael had figured out, the numbers after times five ended in the same numbers as before times five: 2, 4, 6, 8, 10 was the same as 12, 14, 16, 18, 20, only with ones, and then a two, in front. So, all you really had to know was 2, 4, 6, 8, 0. And with five, you just had to know 5, 0, 5, 0, 5, 0 and so on. Nines were fun because you just counted down, like for a rocket launch, on the second number, and you counted up, like in hide and seek, for the first number: 9, 18, 27, 36, 45, 54, 63, 72, 81, 90. Sometimes, after counting 9, 8, 7, 6,

5, 4, 3, 2, 1, 0, Michael would whisper, "Blast off." The other multiplications were harder, but fun. Three just went 3, 6, 9, then dropped one to go 2, 5, 8, then dropped another to go 1, 4, 7 and 0. The four dropped down two: 4, 8, then 2, 6, 0, then repeated 4, 8, 2, 6, 0. Six and seven were the hardest, because they jumped all over. At least six repeated itself: 6, 2, 8, 4, 0, then again. Seven was just down three each time: 7, 4, 1, 8, 5, 2, 9, 6, 3, 0.

But Michael could do them all, and when he did, when he had the numbers in his head, he didn't think about anything else. It was like when he was home, cooking, and there was nothing but the next ingredient, the next step, and then the broth roiled around, or the cream soup thickened. But he couldn't do his soups on the bus, and so numbers were the best thing when he didn't want to think about Evelyn, or about his mother, or about Frank, or Mr. Sandori. Or worry about what they were thinking. He was on the sevens, just saying "twenty-*eight*, thirty-*five*, forty-*two*," when he realized Evelyn was staring at him.

"Your stop," she said. "Soup time."

Michael stood up and hurried out the door. He always moved as fast as he could in front of the Express. Mr. Sandori would know he was a hard worker, a "Monday" worker, as his boss said over and over again.

The next day, Tuesday, Frank was driving the bus. Michael pushed himself up the stairs, his change ready in his hand. He put in his coins and told Frank, "I don't work at the Express today. I have to go downtown and switch to the Seventeenth Street bus. I need a transfer."

Frank didn't even look at him, just handed him the transfer slip.

"I'm stocking at Wal-Mart, you know," Michael told him.

Frank frowned and nodded his head. Michael hurried to the back of the bus, to the bench. Michael had ridden the bus all of his life, since they wouldn't let him drive. When he was small, the bus seats were so hard he squirmed in them. Then came plastic seats, at least shaped like someone's bottom. "Not my bottom," he told his mother. Then came the padded seats, the bench in the back like a throne where the King of the Bus could survey his kingdom. On came the orderlies, the office workers, the men who couldn't drive their cars anymore because they'd been drunk too many times, the older school kids the city contracted with the school district to haul, the poor people who would register for unemployment and pretend to look for jobs. If you couldn't work hard enough to *find* a job, Michael remembered his father saying, how could you ever work hard enough to *keep* a job?

Stocking was harder work than cooking soups. At the Express, Mr. Sandori stood over him, watching, and always tasting, but he liked Michael's soups. At Wal-Mart, Mr. Frazier was never happy. He was always saying things like, "Wrong fucking shipment. Wrong fucking shelf. Wrong fucking order. Wrong fucking department." Everything was "wrong fucking," even though Michael could usually get things in the right place before they ran out of merchandise on the shelves. In all his time cooking alphabet soup, Michael had never seen a bad word come to the surface. Michael told his mother, and she said that was because when you considered all the words, there really weren't that many naughty ones. She thought Michael might go all his life without seeing one. She hoped so, she said.

He knew he shouldn't, but sometimes, when he was stocking the shelves, Michael liked to imitate Mr. Frazier, only Michael turned wrong into right. One time, he didn't see a customer through the open space that let her see and hear him from another aisle. He was bringing a handful of toothpaste to the shelves. "Right fucking shipment," he muttered, "and right fucking shelf."

When he saw the look on the woman's face, he dropped the eight thin boxes of toothpaste to his feet. He didn't dare look at her again, so he sat down in his aisle and hoped she'd go to another part of the store. Without reporting him to Mr. Frazier. Sitting there, waiting for her to leave, waiting to see if Mr. Frazier was going to swoop down on him, he realized how much he was surrounded by words and numbers. They were random, really. Sure, they meant something on the bottles of shampoo. The words announced goodness or made recommendations on the box; but there were also odd letters put together on cartons, paper wrappers, plastic – made-up names that had come to mean something to certain customers. The numbers, too, were sometimes random, sometimes meant something: under bar codes, in percentages, or parts of some formula. When Michael looked around him, from shelf to shelf, from one side of the aisle to another, the numbers and words were just numbers and words, surrounding him, surfacing in his mind like the letters and words of his alphabet soup, circulating through his brain like the multiplication tables he concentrated on so hard to shut everything else out.

Michael sat for a long time, mesmerized, overwhelmed by the shapes of words and letters and numbers, the colors and pictures, until Mr. Frazier swooped down on him. Michael couldn't say anything for a second, then stammered, "I . . . dropped . . . these." He pointed to the boxes at his feet. "Toothpaste," he said.

"So pick them up and put them on the fucking shelf," said Mr. Frazier. "We don't pay you to sit on your ass."

Michael got to his knees. "You pay me to work hard," he said. His hands found the toothpaste. "And I work hard. I'm working hard."

"Good," said Mr. Frazier. It was the same way Mr. Sandori said "good," when Michael had taken the moldy cheese and cut off the fuzzy gray, and picked away at the crushed parts of the old broccoli head, and made a steaming pot of "Home-cooked Broccoli-Cheese Soup." It was the same "good" that Frank said when Michael got on the bus and told Frank where he was going that day, the Express or Wal-Mart.

Michael knew Frank didn't like him. Maybe Mr. Sandori and Mr. Frazier didn't like him, either. He knew Evelyn liked him. She didn't say "good" like she meant "goodbye" or "good riddance" or "good God!" And he thought that next time he got on the bus he'd tell Evelyn that he liked her, too.

The next day, Wednesday, when the bus pulled up to his stop, and Michael saw that Evelyn was driving, his mouth began to bubble with words. He forgot to look at his watch and talk to her about time. Because he just stumbled up the steps, and his tongue felt like his feet. Like stirring alphabet soup: the sounds, the letters, the words were all there, but they were all jumbled, random, confused. Michael had practiced saying, "I like it when you drive the bus. You're a good driver. I like you, Evelyn."

Instead, he fumbled his coins into the box and sat down beside her. He started in on his multiplication tables, trying to make them keep going up, past ten. Eleven and twelve were too easy. Thirteen was harder, but Michael knew cards, and since the deck was just four hands of thirteen, he could get started. But he was having trouble moving higher than fifty-two.

"Why are there fifty-two cards in a deck?" he asked Evelyn without even thinking.

"How should I know?" She eyed Michael in the rearview mirror. "It must go way back. Not to America, right? Because we don't have the Kings and Queens and stuff here."

"Or Aces or Jacks or Jokers," said Michael.

"We've got jokers," said Evelyn. "You know what Frank did? Got my route sheet. Between two sheets he wrote me a note. He thinks I ought to marry him."

Michael threw his eyes out the window to begin counting something.

"Can you imagine that?" asked Evelyn, but Michael said nothing. They were almost to his stop, downtown, near the Express.

Michael stood up. Evelyn put on her signal, began to move the bus to the curb. "No," said Michael.

"No what?" asked Evelyn.

"I can't imagine that," said Michael. "Frank doesn't like the bus. Not like you like the bus."

"What're you cooking today?" Evelyn asked him. The bus groaned to a stop and she jerked the door lever.

"Wednesdays are home-baked bread days," said Michael. "To go with home-cooked soup." He smiled, in spite of himself.

"You're a joker, too," said Evelyn.

Michael beamed. "I'm going to make you alphabet soup." He hopped off the bus.

"Work hard today," Evelyn shouted after him.

If he couldn't tell her he liked her, he could show her. So on Thursday, when he got on the bus, he had a container of alphabet soup. The night before, he'd sorted through the letters and made sure the soup didn't have Frank's letters in it. He left A and N because they were in his name and Evelyn's. But he rejected F and R and K. He noticed those spare letters sitting together on the counter, how they were all alike, a line on the left, with two lines coming out, like freaky little legs. The R was just an F with the little lines joined together. In the K, the little legs stuck out, away from each other, like a cheerleader

121

doing the splits. Really, they were skinny little letters, like Frank. Michael was glad they weren't in his soup.

"For you," he said to Evelyn. He handed her the huge Tupperware bowl, its lid carefully burped over and over before he'd left his house. "It's alphabet soup," he said.

She sat still, looked out the window and sighed. "I'm not supposed to accept any gifts," she said when Michael did not move. "It's company policy, Michael."

"It's our soup," Michael said.

"Go sit," said Evelyn. She reached forward and pulled on the door handle. The door burped shut, sounding like amplified Tupperware.

Michael took his usual seat, right behind her. His day was not starting right. Not after he'd worked so hard the night before: sorting alphabet noodles, making a broth of chicken stock and tomatoes, adding chopped onion and celery and carrots and garlic, and thickening it at the last minute with cornstarch and a little cream. With his special spices, the whole house smelled warm and delicious.

Michael knew what he had to do. "It's our soup," he said again. He popped the lid and waited until he knew Evelyn could smell it. "Now you have to take it," he said.

"I can smell it," Evelyn said. "Thanks for the gift, but that's all I can do. Just smell it."

"You can come have dinner at my apartment. I've got lots more soup."

"I can't," said Evelyn. "Now put the lid on that soup before you make everybody on the bus cranky with hunger."

Michael burped the Tupperware.

"You need a transfer today?" asked Evelyn.

"It's Thursday. I'm working at Wal-Mart." Then, under his breath, he whispered, "Wrong fucking soup. Wrong fucking day."

"You're not to talk like that on my bus," Evelyn said quietly, just to Michael.

"Mr. Frazier, he says bad things all the time. So does Mr. Sandori. But nobody lets me."

"Frank's a cusser, too," said Evelyn. "Must be the whole male half of the population. All of them cussing away."

"My mother doesn't want me to cuss," said Michael. "But I get mad. You won't let me give you soup. Or come eat with me. I make good soups."

"Well, your soup smells good. Maybe I'll talk to Frank. Maybe we could have some soup with you sometime. The two of us."

"The three of us," said Michael. He sounded to himself like his mother, impatient. "You'd be with me, too." He looked away. He'd never talked like that to Evelyn before.

"Yeah, the three of us," said Evelyn. She handed Michael his transfer as he stood up, readying himself to get off at his stop. Evelyn glided to a halt, and, as Michael climbed down the steps, said, "Sorry about the soup."

Friday was an Express day, and Frank was driving when the bus pulled up to Michael's stop. Michael didn't look at him, just deposited his coins in the waiting glass box. Frank reached for the transfers. "Express," Michael said, and moved as quickly as he could toward the back of the bus.

He sat on the throne and watched Frank drive: impatiently, with jerks and fast stops. Before their stops, nobody stood up until the bus was completely still. With Evelyn, you could start toward the door half a block from where you wanted to get off. Michael could not understand why Evelyn would want to marry Frank. Surely he'd treat her like he did the bus, frustrated, jerky, like she was a thing, not a person.

Michael was glad he didn't have to drive. Making soups was completely different from driving, especially the way Frank drove. Only men talked to Frank, or seemed to understand the way he drove the bus.

Michael reached up and pulled the cord to let Frank know his stop was soon. He never did that with Evelyn, because she always knew. After the bus pulled to the curb, Michael started down the aisle. He would go out the side door. But then he heard a voice, and saw that Frank was turned sideways in his driver's seat. "What?" asked Michael.

"You making those home-cooked soups today?" Frank shouted.

"Monday and Friday," said Michael. "I work hard."

"You got a lunch break?"

"Mr. Sandori has me eat my lunch late, not until one thirty, that's how hard I work." Michael started down the steps.

"Evelyn said to tell you we'd be there. At one thirty. To eat one of your soups." Frank turned back around in his seat.

Michael looked at his watch. He knew time was passing, but his watch just seemed like something dark on his wrist, like a funny bracelet. "At one thirty," Michael said, and then he hurried down the steps and heard the door crash closed after him.

Michael could barely work. He thought and thought about a plan. He had done one thing right. He'd put the large Tupperware bowl of special alphabet soup in the cooler at Wal-Mart, then transferred it to the Express on the way home. He would serve them that, with bread. He'd pay for the bread and for drinks. Even for Frank. All morning, his watch moved so slowly Michael wondered if the battery were running down. He had to count things to make the time pass at all, and then he couldn't concentrate. Mr. Sandori yelled at him twice, once because he was afraid the soup wouldn't be ready by ten thirty, and another time because Michael was wasting too much of the rotten onions from Monday's shopping trip.

Michael was glad he had the alphabet soup, because by Fridays, when he had to cook the weekend soups, ingredients were stale and limp. The onion soup would be watery, and Mr. Sandori liked it with too much salt. "Makes it taste like it's got more beef broth in it," Mr. Sandori said. "Taste it."

Michael did, but he didn't like it. "Good," he said. "Everybody's going to like it."

"What's that goddamned Tupperware doing in my cooler?" Mr. Sandori asked later.

"My lunch," said Michael. "And my friends from the bus are coming. For my lunch break. Can I serve it to them out at a table?"

"We'll be slow by then," said Mr. Sandori.

"Like me?" Michael asked. It was one of their jokes.

Mr. Sandori smiled. "I don't give a rat's ass how slow you are, as long as you don't slow down the soup. I want to serve at ten thirty."

The soup was ready, and then customers crowded in, and from eleven thirty to one o'clock Michael was spreading garlic butter on Texas toast, counting the slices. Almost a record day. By one o'clock he'd prepared 173, which times one was 173, times two was 346, times three was easy, because you just add 346 and 173 to get 519, and times four was just times two twice, or 692, and on and on Michael went, trying to calculate up to times ten, just add a zero, and then go back down, and back up and back down, so that the time would pass until Evelyn and Frank came and ate his alphabet soup, the one with no F, no R, no K. He thought that time would never come. And he was right.

Michael dreaded the arrival of Monday's bus, but he had to get to work. If Frank was driving, Michael wasn't going to say a word, because probably Frank had been making a joke, and Michael had long ago tired of being the butt of anyone's joke. If Evelyn was driving, Michael didn't know what he'd say. He thought he might tell her about what he'd been trying to get someone to do with him. Maybe she would. If she wasn't part of the joke, too.

And then the bus was barreling down the street, fast, like Frank was the driver. He saw that Frank *was* the driver. Michael had to force himself up the steps. He saw how big his shoes were, bigger than anybody else's on the bus, probably. "Big head, big feet," his mother always said. "At least you're the same top to bottom."

Michael dropped the coins in the glass box, and saw Frank's thin hand flip the switch so the coins would drop below, out of sight. That's where Michael wanted to be, too. He started down the aisle, moving for the back as quickly as he could. Then he heard Evelyn's voice, calling his name. He turned, and saw that she was sitting where he would be, if she were driving.

"Come here," Evelyn said, and patted the seat next to her.

Michael did as he was told. Frank jerked the bus away from the curb, and Michael almost fell, but he held onto the seat backs and pulled his way forward. He sat next to Evelyn. His leg touched her leg for a second, and he shifted toward the aisle to give her room.

"Frank has something he wants to tell you." Evelyn spoke loud enough for both Frank and Michael to hear.

"Not something I want to tell you," said Frank, "but something I'm *going* to tell you." He twisted his head around once, but he didn't look Michael in the eye. "I made that up about Evelyn saying we'd meet you at the Express. I probably shouldn't've done it. Hope it didn't make trouble for you."

"Frank's trying to say he's sorry," said Evelyn.

"I'm saying I hope it didn't put you out," said Frank without looking behind him.

Evelyn put her arm across the seat, above Michael's shoulder. She said, just to him, "I know it put you out, and he knows it, too. He should be saying he's sorry."

"It's okay," said Michael. He knew one thing, and he'd learned it from years and years on the playground and in parks and on playing fields and in job training and on buses and everywhere else in his life: if you just said it was okay, people might leave you alone. And, if you were Michael, you were lucky if people left you alone. Michael started to get up.

"Stay here," said Evelyn. "Tell us about the soup. Tell me what we missed on Friday."

Since Frank wasn't turning around to look at him, or at Evelyn, Michael decided to pretend Frank wasn't there. "It was *our* soup," he said.

"Our soup?" Evelyn asked.

"The soup I tried to give you on Thursday. I took it to the Express on the way home. It was a special soup, alphabet, but without the letters F or R or K."

"Why not those letters?"

"I didn't want it to be able to spell out 'Frank.' It wasn't for him. It was for you. I like you. But Frank's mean, and he plays tricks and I'm glad I didn't have to eat with him on Friday, and that's why it's okay. He can't even drive a bus as good as you can." Michael stood up then, because he was afraid of what Frank would say.

But then he did know, because Frank was muttering, "Sonofabitch, sonofabitch, he left me out of the alphabet. What am I going to do?" Frank laughed out loud.

Michael swayed all the way to the back of the bus and sat on his throne. His stop would come soon, and he'd be done. He didn't care now. He'd told Evelyn that he liked her, and he'd told Frank he didn't like him, and that's more than he could usually say. He watched Evelyn and Frank talking, even heard their raised voices. Frank hit the steering wheel once, and everybody on the bus heard the really bad word, "shit."

Evelyn came and sat next to Michael. "Shit," she said. "I shouldn't say that, but I don't know what to say."

"My mom always says don't say anything, but then you might be quiet all your life."

"Yeah, and that's a long time," said Evelyn. "And to think I almost said I'd marry him."

"You're not going to?" asked Michael.

"I'm not the marrying type," said Evelyn. "I don't like people to crowd me."

"Will you do something with me, right now, before the bus gets to the Express?"

"Depends on what it is," said Evelyn.

"You just have to count," said Michael. "Count down, like from ten to zero, only start with nine instead of ten and don't say zero. And pause just a little after each number."

"Why?"

"Because I don't know if it will work, but I've thought about it for a long time. Because if I count up, while you count down, and if I say 'tee' in front of my numbers, something should happen."

"What?" Evelyn looked suspicious, like Frank might look.

Michael smiled at her. "You'll see. It's just numbers. It's nothing bad. Start with nine."

"Nine," said Evelyn, and as soon as the sound was out of her mouth, Michael made the sound "tee," and Evelyn said "eight" and Michael said "tee-one," and "seven" and "tee-two," and "six" and "tee-three," and "five," "tee-four," and "four," "tee-five," and "three," "tee-six," and "two," "tee-seven," and "one," "eight," and "nine," Evelyn said, and Michael said nothing.

"What did we just do?" asked Evelyn.

"Almost," said Michael. "We almost did it." He stood up. He pulled the cord over his head to signal his stop.

"Almost did what?" asked Evelyn.

"The numbers. We were doing the nines backwards. Now, you count up. You'll see. Only instead of two, say 'twen' and instead of three say 'thir.'"

"This is too crazy," said Evelyn. "The nines?"

"The multiplication tables. The nines."

"Oh," said Evelyn. "The nines. Like nine and eighteen and twenty-seven . . ." And she stood up, too, because the bus was stopped. She walked with Michael to the front. When they were just behind Frank, she said, "Nine," then "Eighteen," then "twen."

And Michael said, "Tee-seven."

And Evelyn, "Thir."

And Michael, "Tee-six."

"Four," and "tee-five."

"Fif," and "tee-four."

"Six," and "tee-three."

"Seven," and "tee-two."

"Eight," and "tee-one."

"Nine," and "tee."

"What in the Sam Hill is nine tee?" asked Frank.

Evelyn began to laugh, so loud that Michael could laugh, too. And the two of them laughed with each other until Frank stood up. "I don't see what's so goddamned funny," he said.

"Nine tee is the number," said Evelyn. "The *number* ninety, Frank. That's what's so funny."

"Nine," she said, and Michael said "tee." And they went back down the nines, getting better and better.

When they were finished, Frank just shook his head. "You guys ought to join the circus or something. You're so funny."

"My cat's funny," said Michael. "I took some soup home because you weren't there to eat it on Friday. But he ate it. He ate a mouse. The mouse that was in the soup."

"You put a mouse in the soup?" asked Frank.

"Sure," said Evelyn. "And a cat, and a lizard, and an eyeball."

"M, O, U, S, E," said Michael. "They were the noodles of the alphabet."

"Right," said Evelyn. "And your cat ate *that* mouse?"

"No more mouse," said Michael. "No more lizard or eyeball, either. We ate them all. Goodbye, Frank," said Michael. "If I'd put your name in the bowl, my cat would have eaten you." Michael laughed again, and Evelyn joined him.

"Goodbye," Evelyn called after Michael.

He stepped off the bus, but he waited on the sidewalk, wondering if Evelyn might get off the bus, too. He saw her talking to Frank, whispering in his ear.

Frank frowned and turned red. "Don't leave, Evelyn," Frank said, only it wasn't asking, it was telling, and Michael knew then that Evelyn would come down the steps.

She did. "So," she said, "have you tried other numbers?"

"I don't think they'd work as well," said Michael.

"Have you tried?" asked Evelyn.

"No," said Michael. "I don't have anyone to try them with."

"Don't get the wrong idea," said Evelyn. "But someday I'll come for lunch. We'll try some more numbers. Just as friends."

"What will Frank say?"

"Nothing," said Evelyn. "I think your cat ate his tongue."

Michael laughed. "I bet he did. I bet there was a tongue in that soup, too."

"Get to work," said Evelyn.

"I work hard," said Michael.

"I know you do," said Evelyn. "I know you do."

The Bocce Brothers

Without a doubt, the twin Undorte brothers, Peter and John, are the finest bocce players in America, and perhaps the world. Many people wonder how they came to play bocce, where and how they learned, what gives them that keen edge in every bocce competition.

"We love the game," Peter will say, when asked.

"It's fun. Why else play it?" John will add, shrugging his shoulders. They are as impenetrable as they are unbeatable, as inscrutable as they are invincible to their opponents. They are, simply, bocce giants.

But even giants were once boys, and victory exists only because the world is full of defeats. One thinks of "The Bocce Brothers" of the headlines, the tournament trophies, the cash prizes, and one thinks of a magical world, untouched yet by defeat. But how magical is the world? How free of defeat?

1950. Each Sunday after Mass, the Undorte brothers ran home to their pigeons. After being cooped up in the sanctuary, after being fed the host by Father Bellefronte, after the endless hymns and offerings and recessions, the brothers were eager to let their birds loose to sail on steady wings through the Pennsylvania sky.

Their grandmother, Beatrice Undorte, always knew where to find them. "Come, my orphans of the Lord," she would say. "It is time for your bocce."

And so they fed the pigeons who had returned, and locked them into the cages, and spread the bocce balls at one end of the narrow backyard.

"Why do you always call us orphans of the Lord?" asked Peter, throwing the small orange pallino, the target ball, into the spotty grass.

"Because the Lord saw fit to take your mother in her childbirth. He took her life, but He gave her, and you, a gift. My boys, though you have no mother, you know that twins are never alone in the world."

"And where is our father?" asked John as Peter threw the first of his balls.

Because the question upset his brother, he always saved it until Peter was throwing his first ball, a green one, trying to roll it close to the pallino.

"Do not think about a father," said their grandmother. "Is it not enough that he abandoned your mother? That he abandoned you? Has he come for you in twelve years?" Beatrice strode out into the lawn. "Peter, you must throw again. Remember, short is better than long on the first throw. Cover the pallino. Make John throw many balls trying to come closer, or trying to knock you away." She leaned down and picked up Peter's ball. She carried it back and handed it to him. "Now be calm. This is a game of the mind. Your body must serve your mind, and do as your mind tells you."

"Do what *your* mind tells me," said Peter.

"And is there anything wrong with my mind?" Beatrice Undorte folded her arms over her chest and looked at the sky. A last pigeon returned from its release. "Have I not taught you well?" She seemed to be asking the bird.

Peter threw the green ball again. His grandmother smiled as it came to rest three inches in front of the pallino.

John had to move the width of the yard even to see the orange target ball behind Peter's first throw.

His grandmother moved with him, stood at his shoulder. "You can come closer, John," said his grandmother. "Just edge past Peter's ball. Long will be better than short, because you can always hit the pallino back, towards the long balls."

John calmed himself and concentrated. But his red ball hit a clump of grass and veered wildly to the side.

"Like this," said his grandmother, picking up a red ball. She studied the grass, then seemed to disappear into her mind. She released the ball almost as though she were dropping it, but it rolled smoothly, and with distance, and came to rest just to the left of the pallino, perhaps two inches away. It was closer than Peter's ball, and so Peter would have to throw until one of his green balls was closer again.

"What will you do?" his grandmother asked him.

Peter looked at the configuration of balls. He stood up straight. "I'll get closer to the pallino, on the opposite side as your ball. Or I'll knock your ball away. Or hit my own ball closer to the pallino." He recited his options as though they were a catechism.

"You have three balls still," his grandmother reminded him. "The game is not to be won with each throw. Only the final throw determines the points."

Peter picked up the second of his green balls. His throw went astray, crossing the sidewalk and nearly hitting the pigeon just landed in the yard. The pigeon moved its fluid head, bobbing up and down, examining the ball.

Peter's third ball stopped short. His last ball came to rest in front of the red ball his grandmother had thrown.

"Short," she said scornfully.

"Forgive me, for I have sinned," said Peter.

"A sin, yes," she said. "You have short balls already. A long ball now would protect you. John could hit your ball into the pallino. Once the pallino is down the court, he can score two points or more simply by throwing his balls past yours. Short protects the pallino, long protects the score. Always have short and long by the game's end."

"John can't throw *that* well," said Peter.

"Nor can you," said his grandmother. "Remember, you are not playing John and what *he* can do. To improve, you play an imaginary opponent. Think of what your *best* opponent could do. This will help you when you play someone who not only knows *what* to do, but *how* to do it."

"We know what to do," said John.

"But we'll never know how," said Peter.

"Nonsense, boys," said Beatrice Undorte. "You are almost men. Someday, when you go to the Bocce Club, you will know more than many men. I have taught you well. Now, John, throw your balls, and score points."

And so they played, each Sunday, until Beatrice Undorte went inside to fix dinner, until she called them to eat. Then they played until she made them stop in the late afternoon, before their grandfather might return from the American Sons of Columbus, where he drank wine, and shot his gun, and played his bocce.

On their thirteenth birthday, the Undorte brothers sat at the kitchen table with their Grandfather Romano. The old man took slurping sips of very black coffee and studied the newspaper in front of him. Grandmother Beatrice kneaded dough for the sweet rolls she and her grandsons would eat after Mass. She muttered, folding both hope and bitterness, like the wine-soaked raisins, into the pastry.

As always, when Beatrice was finished kneading, and had covered the rolls with a towel, she pointed a floured finger at her husband, "So you are too good for Our Lord? You have no sins to confess?"

Romano looked up from the newspaper. "Not to Father Bellefronte," he said.

She scowled. "So you must drink your wine at the Sons of Columbus? And shoot your gun on Sunday? And lose games of bocce?"

This was the litany of Romano Undorte's sins. He listened much as though his wife were reciting a rosary, each bead a grievance, and the saying of each a comfort to both of them.

"And on the birthday of your grandsons?" Beatrice asked.

He finished his coffee and took his cup to the sink. He passed by Beatrice, patted her shoulder, and brushed her ear with a kiss. She tried to shrug him away, but she did not touch him with her floured hands. Romano Undorte turned to his grandsons, Peter and John, who stared down into their cups of milk, light brown with the coffee he had poured in them. "You must come to the club," he said, as he did each week. "We need pigeon boys."

"Get on with you," said his wife. "It is enough that you do as *you* must do."

"Wish Father Bellefronte well," he said. "Tell him I miss him on the bocce court."

"Don't joke with me," she said.

"Let them come after Mass," said their grandfather. "They are young men today, and it is a day for sun. For warmth, as we knew in Italy. Do not deprive them because the club is only for men."

"Any of those men – I could beat *any* of them at bocce," said Beatrice Undorte.

"You have trained these boys well. Is it not time for them to see what they might do?" asked Romano Undorte.

The Undorte brothers did not dare look at their grandmother, nor say a word. If she saw their eager eyes, heard their lips bubble with begging, she would say, as she always did, "I am not ready to lose these orphans as I have lost you. As I have lost everyone." Each boy saw his own dark eyes reflected in the mug of milk in front of him. Those eyes might have been two other people, perhaps a mother and a father, looking up into the room.

After Mass, Father Bellefronte stood at the door wishing his parishioners well. Beatrice Undorte gathered her breath and said, in one long sigh, "Is it right for the Sons of Columbus to mock the Lord's day, that our men find their way to the club instead of staying with their families?"

Father Bellefronte looked at Peter and John, at how the space between their shoes and the bottoms of their Sunday pants grew each week, at how their suit coats pinched their seventh-grade shoulders. The priest smiled at the boys. He folded his hands. "Señora Undorte, you have been a faithful wife, a fine mother and grandmother. The world takes even boys, and grows them into men."

The old woman scowled. "Into American Sons of Columbus?"

"Perhaps into sons, yes, rather than grandsons," said the priest, as the recessional line, swelling behind them, pushed Beatrice Undorte and her grandsons out the door and into warm sunshine.

"Why don't you like Father Bellefronte?" Peter asked his grandmother.

"He is our priest," she said. "I do not speak ill of him."

"But you don't like him," said John.

"He hears our confessions," said Peter.

"He hears many things," said Beatrice Undorte. "He knows the sins of every man. And yet he remains silent. I know he is a priest, but some things should be known to human ears as well as to divine ears."

"What things?" asked John.

"Shut up," said Peter. He slugged his brother in the arm.

"Shut up yourself," said John, making a fist.

"Yes," said Beatrice Undorte. "We are all shut up by what we do not know, and what no one will tell us."

Peter ran away, down the street.

John followed him. "What is she talking about now?" he asked his brother.

"Don't be a dummy," said Peter. "She's talking about our father. Father Bellefronte probably knows who he is. If anybody would know, it'd be him."

Once home, the boys devoured the pastry. Each raisin was sweet with sunlight, swollen with wine. They thought about the American Sons of Columbus: a sweet swell of promise, then bitter disappointment, week after week. Peter demanded coffee, black.

"So you think yourself a man today?" said his grandmother. She poured an inch of coffee in a cup. She set another cup down for John.

The strong coffee and sweet pastry made their heads spin, delirious, so that when their grandmother spoke to them they had to look at one another to confirm their hearing, that their grandmother had said, "Get off with you now. Go and find your grandfather. Tell him supper is five o'clock. None of you should be late, not on this birthday."

The boys jumped up from the table.

"If you play bocce," said Beatrice Undorte, "you must calm yourselves. You must *win*. I have taught you to *win*."

Peter and John flew from the kitchen, the house, and ran down the steep streets of their small town. The American Sons of Columbus club, with its bocce courts, was on the town's edge, on level ground along the river. The brothers had paced the wooden wall that surrounded it, had pried away knotholes to watch the men sitting on the terrace drinking wine, or loading their guns to shoot, or clapping each other on the back after the thunk of a bocce ball showed that someone had changed the game.

The Undortes walked to the high wooden gate and stood in front, wondering. There were no handles, latches, knobs; no way to pull the huge wooden doors open. Peter knocked. Then John pounded with his forearm. They looked at each other, and around the lot behind them. There were a few cars, but most men walked to the club. They put their ears to the wood of the doors and heard men inside, some of them speaking to each other in Italian, which the brothers heard every day but could not always understand.

Before they knocked again, a man strode toward them. He was smiling, his shirt collar open. He wore an old brown hunting jacket patched under the arm and on the shoulder. When he reached the large doors, the brothers stepped aside and watched his finger find a small button under the huge hinge on the left side. After he pushed the button, he smiled at the boys.

"Peter, John, you are here with the permission of Señora Undorte?" he asked.

"Yes, Father Bellefronte," the boys said.

"Today, I am Father Philipe," said Father Bellefronte.

"But Grandfather told Grandmother he misses you at the bocce courts," said Peter.

"And so he does not admit defeat, even at home?" The priest smiled.

The door suddenly swung out. Bellefronte and the Undorte brothers stepped back. In the doorway, a short, fat man, whom the brothers knew only as Frederico, stood wringing his hands. When Father Bellefronte embraced him, Frederico glowed. "And you've made sure the club is all picked up?" asked the priest.

Frederico nodded his head vigorously. Then he saw the Undorte brothers and backed away. Boys were Frederico's nemesis. They spent their days teasing him, or laughing at him, or mocking him, or imitating him as he walked stiffly around town finding everything there was to pick up. The Undorte brothers, too, had tortured Frederico in their way, dropping litter in front of him to watch him descend on it like a bird feeding on crumbs. Once, they tied fishing line to a paper sack and dragged it away from him as he stooped to pick it up. Like a stray dog, Frederico was everywhere in the town, and no boy, and few men, could resist feeling superior to him.

But on this Sunday, with Father Bellefronte clasping his shoulder, his eyes watering with happiness, his pants, with their accumulated grime, shining in the sunlight, Frederico looked somehow blessed. He twisted his head and whispered something to Father Bellefronte.

"Yes," said the priest, "the grandsons of Romano. They have never been inside these walls as you have.

"Peter, John, you must learn from Frederico to treat things with care." And Father Bellefronte, the boys, and Frederico walked into the bright sunlight of the American Sons of Columbus.

"Peter. John." The boys heard their names and saw their grandfather at a table near the bocce courts, a glass of red wine glowing in the sunlight before him. Their grandfather waved them to the terrace. Father Bellefronte patted their backs and started away.

"Philipe," said Romano, and the priest stopped. "We must have our boc-ce." In the sun, Romano's cheeks glowed like the wine in front of him.

"Later, my friend," said Father Bellefronte. He walked away.

"Always later," muttered Romano. "Bellefronte will shoot first," Romano said to his grandsons. "And then you will see some bocce! But as he shoots, you may earn money. Go find Frederico, at the cages." The old man pointed to where the club opened onto the bluffs above the river.

The boys knew where the shooting range was; they had spent afternoons listening to the booming of shotguns, wondering whether to feel more joy as a fluttering bird plummeted down, or as a pigeon suddenly found itself unharmed, and careened up and away, toward the freedom of its life.

They found Frederico, eyes bright, whispering to the caged pigeons. "Our grandfather . . ." Peter began, but Frederico shook his head and looked away from the boys with an exaggerated grimace. He unlatched a cage, reached in and stroked a pigeon's back. His throat warbled as though he were a bird, too. Then, in one quick movement, he clasped his hand around the bird, covering the wings. He closed the cage door and carried the bird to a nearby trap. "Twenty birds," he said, and jerked his head between the cages and the traps.

Peter opened a cage door. The pigeons fluttered, alarmed, and one shat on his hand. At home, Peter never caught his birds, he simply let them loose, to fly and return when hungry. He grabbed a bird by its head and pulled it from the cage. Its flapping wings seemed huge in his hand, and he knew he had to let go of the bird or it would break its neck trying to escape. He let go.

Frederico threw himself against the wall, clasping his hand to his head. He sighed and grunted like a very loud pigeon. He shook his head. "Gentle," he said. "Be *gentle*men. You try." He pointed at John.

John tried to be gentle, tried to find the pigeon that might allow itself to be caught. But when he tired of patience, he grabbed a bird so that one wing fluttered crazily outside his hand, and the other wing beat inside his fist like a huge living heart. He let go, just as Peter had.

Frederico would not look at the boys. He muttered to himself, "Father Philipe, Our Father, Father Philipe, Our Father . . ." as though trying to re-member the Lord's Prayer.

Frederico moved to the cages again. Throat humming, hands stroking, he swooped up another bird and carried it to the traps. "Frederico will cage them and release the traps," said Father Bellefronte, whom neither boy had seen approach. "You boys will work cleanup. Five dollars between you for recovering the birds." He pulled money from his pants pocket, crumpled bills, thin and ragged, like money from the offering at Mass. He found a five-dollar bill. Neither Peter nor John had held anything but a one. "I am ready to shoot, Frederico. You boys wait behind the shed there until you've counted twenty shots." He gave Frederico the five-dollar bill. "Frederico will pay you when the shooting range closes."

The boys counted to twenty as Frederico released the birds. Occasionally, when a bird would not fly from the trap, the boys had to clap their hands, or throw stones at it. But no matter if they flew straight, circled, or put off their flight; once they found the air, Father Bellefronte downed each of them, some just as they found their wings, some as they fluttered out past the dark background of the bluff and into blue sky.

After twenty booming shots, Frederico hissed at the boys, handed them each a burlap bag, and waved them toward the bluffs. They weren't certain what to do. They walked slowly, until Father Bellefronte laughed, and the man he shot against joined him. "Run, my boys," shouted the priest. "Pick up the birds before we shoot another round. If they aren't dead, you must twist their heads."

They ran from bird to bloody bird, squeamish, trying to deliver the bird to the bag without leaving a trace of blood on their fingers and hands. Peter stopped, stooped, and found the tiny legs, the clawed feet where they curled in the dust. The feet, he thought, would be clean. But Father Philipe yelled, "Hurry, Peter!" And, "John, I like to shoot a warm gun!"

Several of the birds fluttered their wings, and both Peter and John had to grasp those small heads and twirl the birds until their necks were broken. Soon, the boys had no choice but to abandon themselves to sticky blood, to loose feathers, to fecal smears. Finally, they found themselves on the opposite side of the range, with twenty birds between them. Father Philipe waved them behind him, and the moment they walked past the shooting line Frederico began to launch more birds. Twenty, again, and Peter and John stopped watching the fluttering attempts to avoid the birdshot. They simply counted, and ran back out for corpses. Counted, and ran for corpses. Counted, and corpses, until three long hours passed, until many men had come to the range to shoot, until the boys were covered with blood.

Finally, Frederico pulled the five-dollar bill from his pocket. Neither boy wanted to reach for it, to dirty it with the offal of pigeons. Finally, Frederico stuffed the bill in Peter's pocket. "Pigeons die," said the shy man. "They have the blessing of Father Bellefronte. They go to heaven." He crossed himself.

Maybe it was Frederico's awkward seriousness, maybe his clownish, gleaming pants, maybe the smear of pigeon droppings on his coat, and on the hand that made the sign of the cross, but Peter bubbled up with laughter, and John joined him, two boys covered in blood falling onto their backs, as though they'd been shot.

Father Bellefronte sat at Romano Undorte's table, taking small sips from a glass of wine. When Romano saw his grandsons approaching, he waved them to him. He poured an inch of wine in each of two glasses. "Sit," he said to Peter and John. "Sit and drink." His own glass was empty, with only a drop of thick burgundy liquid coagulated in the bottom.

The Undorte brothers sat, and lifted the glasses to their lips. The taste was of communion, only warmer, and more pungent, as though Christ's blood had thickened in the sun of the Bocce Club of the American Sons of Columbus.

"These boys are growing well, Romano," said Father Bellefronte.

"They are young men," answered the grandfather. "Old enough to know some things. Learn others. It is time they threw the bocce balls, Father."

"You must teach them," said Father Bellefronte. "And perhaps someday they will be as skilled as you."

"They know much already. Their grandmother has seen to that. They will beat you. Maybe even today. If *I* cannot, then they will. I had no sons. My daughter . . ." He looked at the boys, bloodied and caked with pigeon offal, and thought of the day they were born. "These boys will play as well as any son."

Father Bellefronte stood up in the silence of a warm day. "Let them get the feel of the court, then," he said.

The boys jumped away and ran to an empty court. Peter threw out the pallino, and it skittered down the well-mown, level grass with a speed he could never achieve in the bumpy lot that was his backyard. He overestimated the speed of his first ball, and it stopped far short of the pallino. John threw wildly long, then very short. They threw all their balls, then, out of order, both trying to pretend they were simply learning the court, its longer distance of ninety feet and the slight resistance of smooth, tight grass, grown from seed that had been brought to America from Italy. When they finished, they walked down the court and threw their balls randomly in the other direction. One of Peter's balls kissed the pallino, and Romano Undorte stood up and clapped his hands.

"We will play you, Father," said Peter. "You can teach us what we don't know already."

The priest looked up into the sky, studied it as though he hoped to find a pigeon, as though he wondered if just one, and then two, had escaped his shotgun blasts. "Yes," he said, "let us play bocce."

The priest won the coin toss and chose to throw the pallino first. He gave the boys the choice of ball color, a small thing, except that Peter had always thrown green, and John red, and neither wanted the other color. The brothers discussed, and then argued until their grandfather pulled them aside. "The balls are twins, like you. They are different, but they are the same. You must have confidence in yourselves, and in each other. A team learns what it can do together. You must be a team, and a team cannot care about individual balls, individual throws, individual mistakes. A team must look only at the placement of balls after the last one has been thrown. Do you understand?"

Peter and John nodded, but each waited for the other to give in.

"Only boys are superstitious about color," said Romano Undorte. "Be men, now. Father Bellefronte wants you to start this way, in conflict about what does not matter."

The boys looked at Father Bellefronte. He had taken off his shooting jacket and rolled up his sleeves. He held the pallino in his hand. He smiled at the Undorte brothers, arguing in the fall sunlight, feathers stuck to their knees, a five-dollar bill peeking from Peter's pocket. John breathed deeply, until the thick smell of the birds became the smell of open air, free and clean.

"I will say the colors in my mind," said Romano, "and you boys give me a signal. When you do, I will tell what color was in my head. That way, we choose together." The old man swayed back and forth, alternating the colors in his head. The brothers looked at each other, then counted to three, and held their hands up. "Green," said Romano Undorte. He smiled, and whispered, "That is my lucky color."

"But you said . . ." Peter whined.

Romano Undorte smiled. "Pay no attention now to anything but the game ahead. Pay no attention to anything but the *whole* game, hold it in your head right now, all of it, more than just the first ball, or the first round, more than Bellefronte's pallino toss, his score in the middle, your best and worst shots. You are playing to twelve points, and you must think for all of them."

And so Father Bellefronte threw out the pallino, and followed it with a red ball, three inches to the right of target. And Peter missed getting closer on the left. And John missed getting closer, though he rolled a ball straight at the target ball and came within four inches. Peter managed to knock the priest's ball away, but Father Bellefronte replaced it in a single throw. John did no better than his first ball, and so the priest rolled his last two balls exactly as he'd rolled his first two, and since he had three balls closer than the Undorte brothers' closest ball, he scored three points.

In the next round the boys did no better, and only a last throw by John, knocking two of Father Bellefronte's balls away, kept the priest from scoring four points.

"Five to nothing," said Philipe Bellefronte. "Romano," he called out, "I thought these boys could play bocce."

"They are used to a backyard of clods and pigeon droppings. But I am watching them. Everyone is watching them." Romano spread his arms as though inviting all the men at the club to pay attention to his grandsons. "And they are thinking well," said Romano Undorte. "You will worry when they start learning the court."

Father Bellefronte sighed and threw the pallino again. His first ball came no closer than a foot. Peter covered the pallino with his first throw. A few men stood up from their tables, downed the last wine in their glasses and came to stand at one end of the court. Father Bellefronte threw a ball hard and knocked both Peter's ball and the pallino toward the back of the court. His ball was still farther away, so he rolled again, this time coming within two inches, but to the right. John knocked his ball away and forced him to throw his final ball. Again, he came within two inches, to the right. Peter went for their third ball, but John stopped him. "Let me knock him again," he said, and Peter nodded.

John did as he said he would. The priest's ball rested against the back wall of the court, and the Undorte brothers had at least a point.

"One more," called out Romano Undorte.

Peter nodded, moved inside himself, and threw the ball. He came within an inch of the target ball, and the Undorte brothers had two points for the round.

More men gathered around the court to watch. A few taunted the priest, making fun of him for being bested by boys. But Bellefronte liked the attention. "*Let* them get ahead," he said. "I like a close game."

"You aren't *letting* them," said one old man. "You would love to win twelve to nothing."

"Wait and see," said the priest.

He watched Peter throw the pallino and cover it with his first ball. He knocked Peter's ball away and threw his next ball directly in front of the pallino. John knocked Bellefronte's ball away and Peter found the uncovered pallino once more. Bellefronte tried to knock away Peter's ball but missed entirely. Hoots of derision flew into the air. The priest threw his last ball, nudging Peter's ball, and the pallino. He was not closer than his opponents, but the balls were lined up, Bellefronte's in front, then Peter's, then the target. John could not knock the priest's ball away without endangering the one point the brothers were certain of. And yet they had another ball to throw. Peter and John huddled.

"Just throw it away," said Peter. "We've got one, anyway."

The old men who lined the court muttered among themselves.

"I might be able to get closer, on the side. That's what Grandmother would say to do," said John.

"Can you do it without screwing up my point?" asked Peter.

"It's *our* point," said John. "That's what Grandmother would say. Grandfather, too."

"You're right," said Peter. "So get us another one."

John crouched down and looked across the grass as though to see it the way the ball might. He rose up slightly, bent his body on his thin legs, and let the ball go. The men at courtside cheered even as it left his hand. The ball found the line John wanted it to take, and came to rest just to the right of the pallino.

"Measurement," called the men. One of them brought out a tape and measured, tossing aside the brothers' closest ball, the one that was a certain point, and seeing whose ball was the next closest after that. "The Undorte brothers have a second point," the man called out.

"Five to four," called out Romano Undorte.

Neither the Undorte brothers nor the priest scored more than one point through the next several rounds. The spread of points remained no greater than two, until, finally, the score was eleven to eleven, and Father Bellefronte, who had won the previous round, was set to throw the pallino.

Peter approached him and whispered into his ear. "Do you think you will win the game?"

"If I didn't I would leave the court right now," said the priest.

John came over to listen to his brother.

"Do you want to make a bet?" asked Peter.

"I do not gamble. And you have only five dollars." Father Bellefronte pointed at the five dollars sticking out of Peter's pants pocket.

"I don't want to bet money," said Peter.

"What do you want?" asked the priest.

"I want you to swear that if we win, you will answer any question we ask you, and you will tell us the truth."

"And if *I* win? What will I have from you?"

Peter shrugged his shoulders. He knew the priest did not care about the five dollars, nor about anything else he owned – not bicycle, not marbles, not pigeons.

"We will promise never to bother you with any question, ever again," said John.

The priest moved away from the boys.

"They are making a bet," said an old spectator. "They have the priest now. He is frightened of their wager."

"What will they bet?" asked another.

"Who can know," said a voice.

"The priest is afraid," observed still another.

Father Bellefronte gathered the Undorte brothers to him. "And whatever it is you want to know, if I win you will be content not to ask me about it, to remain silent about it forever, perhaps never to know?"

"Yes," said Peter, "if you give us your oath to answer honestly whatever question we might ask you."

"I will wager," said the priest.

And so Father Bellefronte threw out the pallino. His first throw went to the right, and just past the target ball, but at the last minute found a slope in the court so that it fell back to take position just behind the pallino by only two inches. Peter concentrated hard and followed with his first throw: perfect, directly in line with and kissing the pallino. He jumped for joy.

"No," said an old man. "You must throw once again."

"What?" said Peter and John together.

"We're touching the pallino," said John.

"But you have moved the pallino back and it is touching Father Bellefronte's ball as well."

"Then why isn't it his turn?" asked Peter.

Romano Undorte walked out to examine the balls. He nodded and came back to where his grandsons stood. "The rule says that you must throw until you are *closer* than your opponent. You have done well, but you are not *closer* when it is a tie."

"Don't give them advice," warned Father Bellefronte.

Romano Undorte smiled. "I am simply explaining the rule, Philipe. These boys need no advice. But I will give *you* some." He pulled a handkerchief from his pocket. "Wipe your forehead. The sweat makes you look nervous."

The priest laughed. "John, I believe it is your throw."

John did as the priest, as everyone, expected him to. He threw a ball to scatter all the balls, to break the tie. He knocked Peter's ball, the pallino, and Father Bellefronte's ball toward the back of the court.

"You are lucky," said the priest when the balls came to rest. Peter's ball was a foot from the pallino; Father Bellefronte's was two feet from it. The priest bowled a perfect line toward the pallino, coming to rest directly in front of it, no farther than two inches away.

Peter threw the next ball, and it came to rest to the left of the pallino, perhaps an inch away.

Father Bellefronte threw hard, and his ball crashed into Peter's ball, knocking it all the way to the back of the court. The priest's second ball, the one two inches in front, remained the point.

John picked up the Undorte brothers' last ball. He examined the court and then whispered to Peter. "I can't get it close like you. I'm better at throwing hard."

Peter shrugged his shoulders. "Then throw hard. Knock everything. All the balls are behind Father Bellefronte's ball and the pallino. Let luck decide what should happen."

And so John tossed the last Undorte ball, hard, in a direct line toward the priest's and the pallino. He knocked them both, scattering them toward the back of the court and the other balls. "Please, God," he whispered. The pallino finally came to rest between an Undorte ball and a Bellefronte ball, so equidistant that the old man with the tape measure had to lumber onto the court to see who had the point.

The priest stood with his last ball and waited, confident now, because his was the only ball left, and he had an open shot to the pallino. If his ball, down there on the court, was already close, he would throw his last ball away. If he was not closer, he would come closer with a last throw.

"The Undorte brothers have the point," the old man with the measure shouted. And all the old men cheered. And mocked the priest. And clapped Romano Undorte on the back.

But Father Bellefronte only smiled. He bent, studied the court, rocked back, and released the ball.

Shouts from the sidelines followed that last ball toward the pallino. And though all of the old men prayed for the ball to go astray, it did not. At least not until the last possible moment, when it veered away slightly and stopped short, coming to rest in front of the pallino.

One needs a bird's eye to judge the proximity of balls at such a distance.

Father Bellefronte began the walk down the court, as did the Undorte brothers. The old man with the tape measure walked out, too, amid shouts that the Undortes were closer, or not, or that it must be a tie, to do over.

But before the old measurer of balls could lay out his tape, before the Undorte brothers and Father Bellefronte could come to see what their estimate might be, Frederico, his grimy pants glimmering in the sunlight, swooped down on the court. He faced the priest, and the boys, and the measurer of balls, a wild grin on his face. And then he kicked the contested balls and picked up the pallino and ran away, off the court, over the terrace, out the large wooden door of the American Sons of Columbus, and out into the town. When he arrived at the river, he threw the pallino up, toward the bluff, as though hoping it might fly away. It dropped into the river, as surely as a pigeon would, shot through by Father Bellefronte.

At courtside, the men began to test their memories and argue about who had been closest to the pallino. Most of them agreed that the Undorte brothers had won the game, that the father's ball had been short, that if it hadn't been, Frederico would never have done what he had, to save the honor of the priest to whom he was so devoted.

Finally, Father Bellefronte turned to the Undorte brothers. "I will say that you won, at least for the sake of the wager you made. You may ask your question, and then we will call the score eleven to eleven and play one more round to see who the winner of the game might be."

Peter and John moved close to the priest, facing him, so that when he spoke, he could speak quietly to each of them, in Peter's right ear, and John's left. "You listen to confessions," Peter whispered. "You're not supposed to tell things. But you gave your oath to tell us one thing."

"If you heard our father's confession, you have to tell us. Who is our father?" asked John.

"Or maybe you know from our mother's confession," added Peter.

The priest looked at the boys. He folded his arms over his chest as their grandmother always did when she was thinking about what to do with them. They folded their arms over their chests, as though imitating him. "My sons," he said, "I give you my oath. *I* have heard no confession from the man who might be your father." He looked at Peter. "Nor did your mother ever speak a name in the confessional."

"But our grandmother said you, of anyone, would know," said John.

"You have to know," insisted Peter.

"Boys," he said. "You asked me if I had heard a man's confession. Or if your mother said a name. I have told you the truth." He squeezed their shoulders. "Haven't you much to be thankful for? Your grandparents have given you an excellent home. Your grandmother has taught you bocce better than any man in this town could have. Is it not enough, what you have now? Is it not enough that you are who you are? You are American Sons of Columbus. You are sons of the church. You have each other. These are all great gifts."

He moved even closer to the boys, then, until his voice was only his breath in their ears. "I predict one thing. That someday, you will find your father. On the bocce court. He will be the only one able to beat you, and you will lose gladly to him. Come," he said, "let us finish our game. Someday, you may find your father. And if not, I pray that you will find yourselves."

And so they took a pallino from another court and played a last round. The balls were close, but the Undorte brothers threw short, and Father Bellefronte moved the pallino back, on his last throw, scoring the final point. Only a few of the old men cheered. The Undorte brothers lost with pride.

When Romano Undorte and the Undorte brothers finally found their way home, they were full of wine. Romano told his wife each detail of the game, while the boys sat dreamily in the kitchen. Their grandmother was not happy that they had been beaten by the priest, though she was proud that Father Bellefronte had won by only one point.

Then Peter and John told her what the priest had said, about confessions, about their finding their father. She folded her arms over her chest. "May you never lose again," she said. And she smiled.

The Undorte brothers did not disappoint their grandmother. They played every week at the American Sons of Columbus, and lost to no one. They started representing their club in tournaments near and far, and still they did not lose. Their play, their spirit, became legend. So did the fact that they refused to play any man of the cloth.

Beatrice Undorte has been dead now for many years. The Undorte brothers dedicate each award, each trophy, to her. When they are asked what advice they have, what secret they know for winning, John says, "Have fun," and Peter says, "Always protect with at least one ball short and one ball long," and then they both say, "And never play a priest!" Still, they send a portion of their winnings to the Catholic church in their small Pennsylvania town.

Their American Sons of Columbus club, with its bocce courts, closed in 1960, when too many of the old men had died or taken sick. Someday, when the Undorte brothers retire, they plan to buy the abandoned club, and revive the tired grass, and make it a place where families can come to learn the game. They want young people to feel welcome. When asked, they say, no, it is not odd to build a shrine to their only defeat.